MORE PRAISE FOR

WE THE ANIMALS

"A poetic slideshow . . . So compelling and so beautiful . . . it reads like a kind of shattering crescendo."
— *NBC Weekend Today*

"On the subject of boyhood, *We the Animals* is the best novel since Roddy Doyle grabbed the 1993 Booker Prize for *Paddy Clarke Ha Ha Ha* . . . [Torres] offers pitch-perfect understanding in pitch-perfect prose, tapping powerful veins of sentiment without succumbing to sentimentality."
— *Times-Picayune*

"Torres makes an unforgettable impression . . . Visceral yet elegant prose." — *Entertainment Weekly,* **Shelf Life**

"Torres mesmerizes with the surprising rhythms and word choice of a slam poet." — *Cleveland Plain Dealer*

"A voice whose uniqueness, power and resonance are evident from the very first page . . . [Readers] will have little choice but to conclude that they are hearing something new, something strong and something very self-assured."
— *Washington Post*

"Beautifully lyrical . . . Both poignant and joyous . . . Torres' writing [is] so electric." — *Salon*

"Taut, elegant, lean — and it delivers a knockout . . . Told in a series of scenes that burst open like exploding stars, full of violence and light . . . the brilliantly compressed novel reads as though Torres has been writing it his whole life . . . A kind of ode to the bond of brotherhood."
— *NPR, Weekend Edition*

"Surge[s] with an electric, emotional power the year's big books couldn't match." — *Time Out New York*

"In stark prose, Torres shows us how one family grapples with a dangerous and chaotic love for each other, as well as what it means to become a man." — *O*

"Torres has spilled onto the scene, big beating heart in hand . . . It feels like reading James Agee by lightning strike. Torres writes like this is the only book he has in him. I certainly hope that's not the case."
— *Arkansas Times*

"[*We the Animals*] shouts, beatboxes and flirts; it lulls only to shock awake; it haunts and creeps and surprises . . . [Torres] writes in a voice that combines urgency, brutality and huggable cuteness." — *Forbes*

"Memorable and vivid . . . It's comparable to *The House on Mango Street*, and just as powerful."
— *Dallas Morning News*

"Torres is a literary wunderkind."
— *San Francisco Bay Guardian online*

"Spare and strong . . . Its rough beauty will linger on long after you turn the last page." — *Minneapolis Star Tribune*

"Voracity—material but also emotional—is what animates most of the book's prose . . . Torres has done here what also good novelists who exploit memory do: he has surveyed his entire childhood and extracted its most pigmented impressions." — *Boston Globe*

"A poetic slideshow . . . So compelling and so beautiful . . . it reads like a kind of shattering crescendo."
— *NBC Weekend Today*

"[Torres] is especially good at creating a sense of heightened or supercharged reality." — *San Francisco Chronicle*

"[A] slender debut novel that packs a hard punch."
— *Dallas-News*

"This searing debut novel ensures that Justin Torres is a name we'll be reading for years to come." — *Next Magazine*

"A treasure chest of unforgettable images and haunting, tender moments." — **Granta.com**

"If you love the smell of language and the taste of the perfect syllable, this book is for you." — **Flavorwire**

"Well-crafted like a great martini, coming in smooth with a potent punch." — **The Brooklyn Rail**

"Luminescent . . . It's [this] book, more than any other this year, that I found myself thrusting into people's hands demanding, Read this." — *Band of Thebes*

"Shows such mastery of crafting vibrant, visual, concise prose that it's hard not to fall in love with and want to reread the novel as you find yourself reaching the last sentences."
— *Lambda Literary*

"Extraordinary . . . Torres demonstrates a mastery of prose seldom encountered in first books. An exhilarating beginning." — *Los Angeles Review of Books*

"*We the Animals* is at its best when it exposes the fierce core of love that can slumber in the troubled heart of even the most damaged families. It's also a declaration of the arrival of a significant new voice on the American literary scene."
— **bookreporter**

"Aptly captures the swirling, joyous mess that is brotherhood . . . Fierce in its ability to evoke potent emotion with poetic language and veracious insight."
— *The Pilot* (**North Carolina**)

"[The novel's] brevity masks an emotional impact that few stories of greater length ever manage."
— *American Statesman* (**Texas**)

"Enveloping and fast-paced prose . . . An ultimately haunting and beautiful atmosphere, one like hearing in the distance the moan of a train whistle at midnight." — *ZYZZYVA*

"Gut-wrenching . . . Torres' prose is sparse and exacting, and he knows his characters well." — *Mother Jones*

"Torres had me hooked." — *Iowa City Press Citizen*

"Intimate in its telling, *We the Animals* rings with truth."
— *AARP Viva*

"Pitch-perfect . . . The tension that hovers beneath the surface of these stories vibrates electrically."
— *BookPage*

"Elegant and raw, vibrant and incomplete. Rarely has a writer developed the child's-eye view with such intimate vulnerability and emphatic restraint." — *Bookslut*

"Filled with rich detail, tableau-like scenes, and true-to-life little boy adventures, *We the Animals* is a must-read novel. Torres' evocative language grips the reader."
— *Sacramento Book Review*

"A work beautiful to behold . . . A master of detail and haunting images." — **Ploughshares Literary Magazine blog**

"This is a book that defies categorization, for the content is a shape-shifting many-headed furious god of love . . . [It] leaves the reader with the singular wish to go back to the beginning." — *Huffington Post*

"Only every so often . . . does something this well written come along . . . That such a young author writes so well in his debut novel seems miraculous."
— *New York Journal of Books*

"Torres is a writer to embrace from the start."
— *Star-Ledger* (New Jersey)

"You applaud first novelist Torres's genius ability to twist around and punch you in the gut . . . Highly recommended." — *Library Journal*

"*We the Animals*, can be described in one word—wow."
— *The Hispanic Reader*

"So essential, so focused and concentrated, so taut and fiery and startling, like a cup of maple syrup made from ten gallons of sap, that everything else starts to sound loose and slack . . . For now, we have to settle for rereading the miniature magical universe Torres has created and hope to satisfy our appetite when he follows up this lightning strike of a debut with a second book." — *The Nervous Breakdown*

"Intriguing and beautifully written." — *Publishers Weekly*

"An exquisitely crafted debut novel — subtle, shimmering and emotionally devastating . . . Upon finishing, readers might be tempted to start again, not wanting to let it go."
— *Kirkus Reviews,* **starred**

WE THE ANIMALS

JUSTIN TORRES

MARINER BOOKS
HOUGHTON MIFFLIN HARCOURT
BOSTON   NEW YORK

For my mother, my brothers, and my father
and for Owen

First Mariner Books edition 2012

Copyright © 2011 by Justin Torres

All rights reserved

For information about permission to reproduce selections from this book,
write to trade.permissions@hmhco.com or to Permissions,
Houghton Mifflin Harcourt Publishing Company,
3 Park Avenue, 19th Floor, New York, New York 10016.

www.hmhco.com

Library of Congress Cataloging-in-Publication Data
Torres, Justin, date.
We the animals : a novel / Justin Torres.
p. cm.
ISBN 978-0-547-57672-5   ISBN 978-0-547-84419-0 (pbk.)
1. Family — Fiction. 2. Brothers — Fiction. 3. Upstate New York
(N.Y.) — Fiction. I. Title.
PS3620.O5897W42 2011
813'.6 — dc22   2011009159

Book design by Melissa Lotfy

Printed in the United States of America

DOC 10 9 8 7 6 5 4

4500670183

CONTENTS

Now a boy is of all wild beasts the most difficult to manage. For by how much the more he has the fountain of prudence not yet fitted up, he becomes crafty and keen, and the most insolent of wild beasts. On this account it is necessary to bind him, as it were, with many chains.

— Plato, *The Laws*

WE THE ANIMALS

WE WANTED MORE

W̲E̲ ̲W̲A̲N̲T̲E̲D̲ ̲M̲O̲R̲E̲. We knocked the butt ends of our forks against the table, tapped our spoons against our empty bowls; we were hungry. We wanted more volume, more riots. We turned up the knob on the TV until our ears ached with the shouts of angry men. We wanted more music on the radio; we wanted beats; we wanted rock. We wanted muscles on our skinny arms. We had bird bones, hollow and light, and we wanted more density, more weight. We were six snatching hands, six stomping feet; we were brothers, boys, three little kings locked in a feud for more.

When it was cold, we fought over blankets until the cloth tore down the middle. When it was really cold, when our breath came out in frosty clouds, Manny crawled into bed with Joel and me.

"Body heat," he said.

"Body heat," we agreed.

We wanted more flesh, more blood, more warmth.

When we fought, we fought with boots and garage tools,

1

snapping pliers — we grabbed at whatever was nearest and we hurled it through the air; we wanted more broken dishes, more shattered glass. We wanted more crashes.

And when our Paps came home, we got spankings. Our little round butt cheeks were tore up: red, raw, leather-whipped. We knew there was something on the other side of pain, on the other side of the sting. Prickly heat radiated upward from our thighs and backsides, fire consumed our brains, but we knew that there was something more, some-place our Paps was taking us with all this. We knew, because he was meticulous, because he was precise, because he took his time. He was awakening us; he was leading us some-where beyond burning and ripping, and you couldn't get there in a hurry.

And when our father was gone, we wanted to *be* fathers. We hunted animals. We drudged through the muck of the crick, chasing down bullfrogs and water snakes. We plucked the baby robins from their nest. We liked to feel the beat of tiny hearts, the struggle of tiny wings. We brought their tiny animal faces close to ours.

"Who's your daddy?" we said, then we laughed and tossed them into a shoebox.

Always more, always hungrily scratching for more. But there were times, quiet moments, when our mother was sleeping, when she hadn't slept in two days, and any noise, any stair creak, any shut door, any stifled laugh, any voice at all, might wake her, those still, crystal mornings, when we wanted to protect her, this confused goose of a woman, this stumbler, this gusher, with her backaches and headaches and her tired, tired ways, this uprooted Brooklyn creature, this tough talker, always with tears when she told us she loved us, her mixed-up love, her needy love, her warmth, those mornings when sunlight found the cracks in our blinds and laid itself down in crisp strips on our carpet, those quiet mornings when we'd fix ourselves oatmeal and sprawl onto our stomachs with crayons and paper, with glass marbles that we were careful not to rattle, when our mother was sleeping, when the air did not smell like sweat or breath or mold, when the air was still and light, those mornings when silence was our secret game and our gift and our sole accomplishment — we wanted less: less weight, less work, less noise, less father, less muscles and skin and hair. We wanted nothing, just this, just this.

NEVER-NEVER TIME

W E ALL THREE sat at the kitchen table in our raincoats, and Joel smashed tomatoes with a small rubber mallet. We had seen it on TV: a man with an untamed mustache and a mallet slaughtering vegetables, and people in clear plastic ponchos soaking up the mess, having the time of their lives. We aimed to smile like that. We felt the pop and smack of tomato guts exploding; the guts dripped down the walls and landed on our cheeks and foreheads and congealed in our hair. When we ran out of to-matoes, we went into the bathroom and pulled out tubes of our mother's lotions from under the sink. We took off our raincoats and positioned ourselves so that when the mallet slammed down and forced out the white cream, it would get everywhere, the creases of our shut-tight eyes and the folds of our ears.

Our mother came into the kitchen, pulling her robe shut and rubbing her eyes, saying, "Man oh man, what time is it?" We told her it was eight-fifteen, and she said fuck, still keeping her eyes closed, just rubbing them harder, and then she said fuck again, louder, and picked up the teakettle and slammed it down on the stove and screamed, "Why aren't you in school?"

It was eight-fifteen at night, and besides, it was a Sunday, but no one told Ma that. She worked graveyard shifts at the brewery up the hill from our house, and sometimes she got confused. She would wake randomly, mixed up, mistaking one day for another, one hour for the next, order us to brush our teeth and get into PJs and lie in bed in the middle of the day; or when we came into the kitchen in the morning, half asleep, she'd be pulling a meat loaf out of the oven, saying, "What is wrong with you boys? I been calling and calling for dinner."

We had learned not to correct her or try to pull her out of the confusion; it only made things worse. Once, before we'd known better, Joel refused to go to the neighbors and ask for a stick of butter. It was nearly midnight and she was baking a cake for Manny.

"Ma, you're crazy," Joel said. "Everyone's sleeping, and it's not even his birthday."

She studied the clock for a good while, shook her head quickly back and forth, and then focused on Joel; she bored deep in his eyes as if she was looking past his eyeballs, into the lower part of his brain. Her mascara was all smudged and her hair was stiff and thick, curling black around her face and matted down in the back. She looked like a raccoon caught digging in the trash: surprised, dangerous.

"I hate my life," she said.

That made Joel cry, and Manny punched him hard on the back of the head.

"Nice one, asswipe," he hissed. "It was going to be my fucking birthday."

After that, we went along with whatever she came up with; we lived in dreamtime. Some nights Ma piled us into the car and drove out to the grocery store, the laundromat, the bank. We stood behind her, giggling, when she pulled at the locked doors, or when she shook the heavy security grating and cursed.

She gasped now, finally noticing the tomato and lotion streaking down our faces. She opened her eyes wide and then squinted. She called us to her side and gently ran a finger across each of our cheeks, cutting through the grease and sludge. She gasped again.

"That's what you looked like when you slid out of me," she whispered. "Just like that."

We all groaned, but she kept on talking about it, about how slimy we were coming out, about how Manny was born with a full head of hair and it shocked her. The first thing she did with each one of us was to count our fingers and toes. "I wanted to make sure they hadn't left any in there," she said and sent us into a fit of pretend barfing noises.

"Do it to me."

"What?" we asked.

"Make me born."

"We're out of tomatoes," Manny said.

"Use ketchup."

We gave her my raincoat because it was the cleanest, and we warned her no matter what not to open her eyes until we said it was OK. She got down on her knees and rested her chin on the table. Joel raised the mallet above his head, and Manny squared the neck of the ketchup bottle between her eyes.

"On the count of three," we said, and we each took a number — my number was last. We all took the deepest, longest breath we could, sucking the air through our teeth. Everyone had his face all clenched up, his hands squeezed into fists. We sucked in a little more air, and our chests swelled. The room felt like a balloon must, when you're blowing and blowing and blowing, right before it pops.

"Three!"

And the mallet swung through the air. Our mother yelped and slid to the floor and stayed there, her eyes wide open and ketchup everywhere, looking like she had been shot in the back of the head.

"It's a mom!" we screamed. "Congratulations!" We ran to the cupboards and pulled out the biggest pots and heaviest ladles and clanged them as loud as we could, dancing around our mother's body, shouting, "Happy Birthday! . . . Happy New Year! . . . It's zero o'clock! . . . It's never-never time! . . . It's the time of your life!"

HERITAGE

WHEN WE got home from school, Paps crowded the kitchen, cooking and listening to music and feeling fine. He whiffed the steam coming off a pot, then clapped his hands together and rubbed them briskly. His eyes were wet and sparkled with giddy life. He turned up the volume on the stereo and it was mambo, it was Tito Puente.

"Watch out," he said and spun, with grace, on one slippered foot, his bathrobe twirling out around him. In his fist was a glistening, greasy metal spatula, which he pumped in the air to the beat of the bongo drums.

We stood there in the entranceway to the kitchen, laughing, eager to join in, but waiting for our cue. Paps staked staccato steps across the linoleum to where we stood and whipped us onto the dance floor, grabbing our wimpy arms and jerking us behind him. We rolled our tiny clenched fists in front of us and snapped our hips to the trumpet blasts.

One by one he took us by our hands and slid us between his legs, and we popped up on the other side. Then we wiggled around the kitchen, following behind him in a line, like baby geese.

There were hot things on the stove, pork chops frying in their own fat, and Spanish rice foaming up and rattling the lid. The air was thick with steam and spice and noise, and the one little window above the sink was fogged over.

Paps turned the stereo even louder, so loud that if we screamed, no one would have heard, so loud that Paps felt far away and hard to get to, even though he was right there in front of us. Then Paps grabbed a can of beer from the fridge, and our eyes followed the path of the can to his lips. We took in the empties stacked up on the counter behind him, then we looked at each other. Manny rolled his eyes and kept dancing, and so we got in line and kept dancing too, except now Manny was Papa Goose, it was him we were following.

"Now shake it like you're rich," Paps shouted, his powerful voice booming out over the music. We danced on tiptoes, sticking up our noses and poking the air above us with our pinkies.

"You ain't rich," Paps said. "Now shake it like you're poor."

We got low on our knees, clenched our fists, and stretched our arms out on our sides; we shook our shoulders and threw our heads back, wild and loose and free.

"You ain't poor neither. Now shake it like you're white."

We moved like robots, stiff and angled, not even smiling. Joel was the most convincing; we'd seen him practicing in his room.

"You ain't white," Paps shouted. "Now shake it like a Puerto Rican."

There was a pause as we gathered ourselves. Then we mamboed as best we could, trying to be smooth and serious and to feel the beat in our feet and beyond the beat to feel the rhythm. Paps watched us for a while, leaning against the counter and taking long draws from his beer.

"Mutts," he said. "You ain't white and you ain't Puerto Rican. Watch how a purebred dances, watch how we dance in the ghetto." Every word was shouted over the music, so it was hard to tell if he was mad or just making fun.

He danced, and we tried to see what separated him from us. He pursed his lips and kept one hand on his stomach. His elbow was bent, his back was straight, but somehow there was looseness and freedom and confidence in every move. We tried to watch his feet, but something about the way they twisted and stepped over each other, something about the line of his torso, kept pulling our eyes up to his face, to his broad nose and dark, half-shut eyes and his pursed lips, which snarled and smiled both.

"This is your heritage," he said, as if from this dance we could know about his own childhood, about the flavor and grit of tenement buildings in Spanish Harlem, and projects in Red Hook, and dance halls, and city parks, and about his own Paps, how he beat him, how he taught him to dance, as if we could hear Spanish in his movements, as if Puerto Rico was a man in a bathrobe, grabbing another beer from the fridge and raising it to drink, his head back, still dancing, still stepping and snapping perfectly in time.

SEVEN

I N   T H E   M O R N I N G , we stood side by side in the doorway and looked in on Ma, who slept open-mouthed, and we listened to the air struggle to get past the saliva in her throat. Three days ago she had arrived home with both cheeks swollen purple. Paps had carried her into the house and brought her to the bed, where he stroked her hair and whispered in her ear. He told us the dentist had been punching on her after she went under; he said that's how they loosen up the teeth before they rip them out. Ma had been in bed every day since — plastic vials of pain pills, glasses of water, half-drunk mugs of tea, and bloody tissues cluttered the floor around her bed. Paps had forbidden us to set foot in the bedroom, and for three mornings we had heeded, monitoring her breath from the doorway, but today we would not wait any longer.

We tiptoed to her side and traced our fingers over her bruises. Ma murmured at our touch but did not wake.

It was the morning of my seventh birthday, which meant

winter, but the light glowed in the curtain like spring. Manny walked to the window, pulled the curtain around him, and covered himself so that only his face was visible. One Sunday, because we had begged her to, Ma took us to a church service, and there we saw a painting of men in hoods with clasped hands and eyes lifted upward.

"Monks," Ma had said. "They study God."

"Monks," Manny whispered now, and we understood. Joel draped himself in the sheet that had been kicked to the floor, and I grabbed the other curtain, and like monks we waited, except it was Ma we were studying, her black tangled hair, her shut eyes, and her bloated jowl. We watched the tiny form of her under the covers, a twitch or kick, and the steady rise and fall of her chest.

When she finally woke, she called us beautiful.

"My beautiful baby boys," she said, the first words out of her busted mouth in three days, and it was too much; we turned from her. I pressed my hand against the glass, suddenly embarrassed, needing the cold. That's how it sometimes was with Ma; I needed to press myself against something cold and hard, or I'd get dizzy.

"It's his birthday," Manny said.

"Happy birthday," Ma said, the words slightly tinged with pain.

"He's seven," Manny said.

Ma nodded her head slowly and shut her eyes. "He'll leave me, now he's seven."

"What's that supposed to mean?" Joel asked.

"When you boys turned seven, you left me. Shut yourselves off from me. That's what big boys do, what seven-year-olds do."

I moved both hands to the glass, caught the cold, and pressed it to my cheeks.

"I won't."

"They changed," Ma said, turning her head to me. "Wriggled away when I tried to cuddle them, wouldn't sit still on my lap. I had to let them go — had to harden my heart — they wanted to smash things, to wrestle."

My brothers looked confused but oddly proud. Manny winked to Joel.

"Aw," he said, "it ain't like that."

"Isn't it?" Ma asked.

"I don't want to smash nothing," I said. "I want to study God and never get married."

"Good," Ma said, "then you'll stay six forever."

"That's just stupid," Joel said.

Ma raised a slow hand for silence on the subject.

"Will you get up today?" I asked.

"How do I look?"

"Purple," I said.

"Crazy," said Joel.

"Tore up," said Manny.

"But it's your birthday," Ma said to me.

"But it's my birthday."

She slid the covers down to her waist and brought her hands up to her face, delicately protecting her cheeks, as if a hand might fly through the air at any moment, then she raised herself up, then her feet were on the floor, then she was standing in her green football jersey, with bare legs thin as anything and painted toes.

A brass-handled mirror lay on the bureau, and as soon as Ma raised it to her face, tears came and sat on her eyelids, waiting to fall. Ma could hold tears on her eyelids longer than anyone; some days she walked around like that for hours, holding them there, not letting them drop. On those days she would trace her finger over the shapes of things or hold the telephone on her lap, silent, and you had to call her name three times before she'd give you her eyes.

Now, Ma held the tears and studied her ugliness. The three of us boys started to back out of the room, but she called for me, said she wanted to talk to me about staying six, but she didn't say much beyond that, just looked and looked in that mirror, turning her jaw at different angles.

"What did he do to me?" she asked.

"He punched you in the face," I said, "to loosen up your teeth."

I jumped at the sound of shattering glass. My brothers' two heads instantly appeared back in the doorway, smiling wide, running their eyes from Ma to me, to the broken pieces of mirror, to the spot on the wall where it had been flung, to Ma, to me.

Ma's hands were up protecting her cheeks again, and her eyes were shut. When she spoke, she said each word slow and clear.

"You think it's funny when men beat on your mother?"

My brothers' smiles dropped to frowns; they disappeared again.

I went and wrapped myself back up in the curtain, leaned my forehead against the windowpane. The light reflected back and forth from the white sky to the snow; the light caught in the frost on the window. Outside, it was too bright to focus on any one spot. I opened my eyes as wide as I could, and they burned with light, and I thought about going blind, about how everyone said if you looked right up into the sun, full on, and held your gaze, you'd go blind — but when I tried, I could not blind myself.

Ma sat on the edge of the bed, breathing loud and slow, forgiving me. She called for me to sit on her lap, and I came, and we breathed together. Then Ma started in on my favorite song, about a woman with feathers and oranges, and Jesus Christ walking on the water. My head stretched all the way up to her shoulder, but she rocked me, rocked me, and hummed the words she had forgotten.

"Promise me," she said, "promise me you'll stay six forever."

"How?"

"Simple. You're not seven; you're six plus one. And next year you'll be six plus two. Like that, forever."

"Why?"

"When they ask how old you are, and you say 'I'm six plus one, or two, or more,' you'll be telling them that no matter how old you are, you are your Ma's baby boy. And if you stay my baby boy, then I'll always have you, and you won't shy away from me, won't get slick and tough, and I won't have to harden my heart."

"You stopped loving them when they turned seven?"

"Don't be simple," Ma said. She brushed my hair back from my forehead. "Loving big boys is different from loving little boys — you've got to meet tough with tough. It makes me tired sometimes, that's all, and you, I don't want you to leave me, I'm not ready."

Then Ma leaned in and whispered more in my ear, told me more, about why she needed me six. She whispered it all to me, her need so big, no softness anywhere, only Paps and boys turning into Paps. It wasn't just the cooing words, but the damp of her voice, the tinge of pain — it was the warm closeness of her bruises — that sparked me.

I turned into her, saw the swollen mounds on either side of her face, the muddied purple skin ringed in yellow. Those bruises looked so sensitive, so soft, so capable of hurt, and this thrill, this spark, surged from my gut, spread through my chest, this wicked tingle, down the length of my arms and into my hands. I grabbed hold of both of her cheeks and pulled her toward me for a kiss.

The pain traveled sharp and fast to her eyes, pain opened up her pupils into big black disks. She ripped her face from mine and shoved me away from her, to the floor. She cussed me and Jesus, and the tears dropped, and I was seven.

THE LAKE

ONE UNBEARABLE NIGHT, in the midst of a heat wave, Paps drove us all to the lake. No one wore anything more than a bathing suit, and Ma had us drape towels over the seatbacks to keep our skin from sticking to the vinyl. We drove the long road in silence, as if we were all together in front of the TV, except what we were listening to and watching was the heat.

Ma and I didn't know how to swim, so she grabbed onto Paps's back and I grabbed onto hers, and he took us on a little tour, spreading his arms before him and kicking his legs underneath us, our own legs trailing through the water, relaxed and still, our toes curled backward.

Every once in a while Ma would point out some happening for me to look at, a duck touching down onto the water, his head pulled back on his neck, beating his wings before him, or a water bug with spindly legs that dimpled the lake's surface.

"Not so far," she would say to Paps, but he'd push on,

smooth and slow, and the shore behind would stretch and thin and curve, until it was a wooded crescent impossibly dark and remote.

In the middle of the lake the water felt blacker and cooler, and Paps swam right into a clump of slimy tar black leaves. Ma and I tried to splash the leaves away from us, but we had to keep one arm holding on, so they ended up curling around in our jetty and sticking to our ribs and thighs like leeches. Paps lifted a fistful into the air, and the leaf clump melted through the cracks in his fingers and disintegrated into speckles in the water, and cigarette-size fish appeared and nibbled at the leaf bits.

"We've come too far," Ma said. "Take us back."

"Soon," Paps said.

Ma started talking about how unnatural it was that Paps knew how to swim, as if he was born up here in this hillbilly country, and not six hours south, in Brooklyn. She said that no one swam in Brooklyn. The most water she ever saw in one place was when one of the men from the block would open up the johnny pump and water would rush and pour forth. She said that she never jumped through the spray like the other kids — too hard and mean and shocking — but instead she liked to stand farther down, where the sidewalk met the street, and let the water pool around her ankles.

"I had already been married and pushed out three boys before I ever stepped into anything deeper than a puddle," she said.

Paps didn't say when or where he had learned to swim,

but he generally made it his business to learn everything that had to do with survival. He had all the muscles and the will. He was on his way to becoming indestructible.

"I guess it's opposite with you, isn't it?" Ma called back to me. "You grew up with all these lakes and rivers, and you got two brothers that swim like a couple of goldfish in a bowl — how come you don't swim?"

She asked the question as if she was meeting me for the first time, as if the circumstances of my life — my fumbling, terrifying attempts at the deep end, the one time at the public pool when I had been dragged out by the high school lifeguard and had puked up pool water onto the grass, seven hundred eyes on me, the din of screams and splashes and whistles momentarily silenced as everyone stopped to ponder my bony weakness, to stare and stare waiting for me to cry, which I did — as if it had only just now occurred to Ma how odd it was that I was here, clinging to her and Paps, and not with my brothers, who had run into the water, dunked each other's heads down, tried to drown each other, then ran back out and disappeared into the trees.

Of course, it was impossible for me to answer her, to tell the truth, to say I was scared. The only one who ever got to say that in our family was Ma, and most of the time she wasn't even scared, just too lazy to go down into the crawl-space herself, or else she said it to make Paps smile, to get him to tickle and tease her or pull her close, to let him know she was only really scared of being without him. But me, I would have rather let go and slipped quietly down to the lake's black bottom than to admit fear to either one of them.

But I didn't have to say anything, because Paps answered for me.

"He's going to learn," he said, "you're both going to learn," and no one spoke after that for a long time. I watched the moon break into shards of light across the lake; I watched dark birds circle and caw, the wind lift the tree branches, the pine trees tip. I felt the lake get colder and I smelled the dead leaves.

Later, after the incident, Paps drove us home. He sat behind the wheel, still shirtless, his back and neck and even his face a crosshatch of scratches, some only deep red lines and broken skin, some already scabbing, and some still glistening with fresh blood, and I too was all scratched up — for she had panicked, and when he slipped away she had clawed on top of me. Later, Paps said to her, "How else do you expect to learn?"

And Ma, who had nearly drowned me, who had screamed and cried and dug her nails down into me, who had been more frenzied and wild than I had ever known her to be, Ma, who was so boiling angry that she had made Manny sit up front with Paps and she had taken the middle back, wrapping her arms around us — Ma replied by reaching across me and opening the door as we sped along. I looked down and saw the pavement rushing and blurring beneath, the shoulder dropping away into a gravel pit.

Ma held open that door and asked, "What? You want me to teach him how to fly? Should I teach him how to fly?"

Then Paps had to pull over and calm her down. The three of us boys jumped out and walked to the edge and took out our dicks and pissed down into the ditch.

"She really clawed you up like that?" Manny asked.

"She tried to climb onto my head."

"What kind of . . ." he started to say but didn't finish. He was two years older than Joel and three years older than me. We waited for his judgment, for the other half of his sentence, but he only picked up a rock and hurled it out away from him as far as he could.

From the car, we heard the noises of their arguing, we heard Ma saying over and over, "You let me go. You let me go," and we watched the big trailers haul past, rumbling the car and the ground underneath our feet.

Then Manny laughed and said, "Shit, I thought she was gonna throw you out of the car."

And Joel laughed too; he said, "Shit. I thought you were gonna *fly*."

When we finally returned to the car, Ma sat up front again, and Paps drove with one hand on the back of her neck. He waited until the perfect moment, until we'd settled into silence and peace and we were thinking ahead to the beds waiting for us at home, and then he turned his head to the side, glancing at me over his shoulder, and asked, all curious and friendly, "So, how'd you like your first flying lesson?" And the whole car erupted in laughter.

But the incident itself played and played in my mind, and at night, in bed, I could not sleep for remembering. How Paps had slipped away from us, how he looked on as we flailed and struggled, how I needed to escape Ma's clutch and grip, how I let myself slide down and down, and when I opened my eyes what I discovered there: black-green murkiness, an underwater world, terror. I sank down for a long time, disoriented and writhing, and then suddenly I was swimming — kicking my legs and spreading my arms just like Paps had shown me long before, and rising up to the light and exploding into air, and then that first breath, sucking air all the way down into my lungs, and when I looked up the sky had never been so vaulted, so sparkling and magnificent. I remembered the urgency in my parents' voices, Ma wrapped around Paps once again, and both of them calling my name. I swam toward their bobbing mass, and there under the stars, I was wanted. They had never been so happy to see me, they had never looked at me with such intensity and hope, they had never before spoken my name so softly.

I remembered how Ma burst into tears and Paps celebrated, shouting as if he was a mad scientist and I a marvel of his creation:

"He's alive!"

"He's alive!"

"He's alive!"

US PROPER

WHEN WE WERE brothers, when we were all three together, we made a woman. We stacked up on one another's shoulders and wrapped ourselves in Ma's long winter coat. Manny was the bottom, the legs, and Joel was the stomach, and I was the lightest, so I was the woman's head. We used a ladder to keep from tipping over, but Manny's knees buckled under our weight, so we had to lie down on the ground and do it that way; we were a fallen woman who could not get back up, a helpless woman, flat on her back.

When we were brothers, we were Musketeers.

"Three for all! And free for all!" we shouted and stabbed at each other with forks.

We were monsters — Frankenstein, the bride of Frankenstein, the baby of Frankenstein. We fashioned slingshots out of butter knives and rubber bands, crouched under cars, and flung pebbles at white women — we were the

Three Bears, taking revenge on Goldilocks for our missing porridge.

The magic of God is three.

We were the magic of God.

Manny was the Father, Joel the Son, and I the Holy Spirit. The Father tied the Son to the basketball post and whipped him with switches while the Son asked, "Why, Paps, why?"

And the Holy Spirit? The Holy Spirit hovered and had to watch — there and not there — waiting for a new game.

When we were three together, we spoke in unison, one voice for all, our cave language.

"Us hungry," we said to Ma when she finally came through the door.

"Us burglars," we said to Paps the time he caught us on the roof, getting ready to rappel — and later, when Paps had us on the ground and was laying into Manny, I whispered to Joel, "Us scared," and Joel nodded his chin toward Paps, who was unfastening his belt, and whispered back, "Us fucked."

When we were three together, we stuck our fingers into each other's eyes and pulled chairs out from underneath. The Stooges were three, the Chipmunks. We pinched our noses and sang Chipmunk Christmas carols. We perfected the human pyramid — not the lazy, kneeling pyramid, but the standing kind. We took turns at being world champions, one paraded on the shoulders of the other two, blowing kisses and shaking fists.

We were the Three Billy Goats Gruff crossing the bridge; we were the trolls that lived under the bridge. But after we learned about sex — after Ma sat us down on the carpet and opened the encyclopedia to "Reproductive Systems," after she showed us cross-section diagrams of penises and vaginas and explained how they fit, after all that — we played a new game. No one had explained sex to Ma when she was a kid — not the nuns at school and not her own mother. So when she asked Paps, "Can't I get pregnant from this?" Paps had lied; he had laughed and asked, "This?" And then there was Manny, all up in Ma's stomach, growing, heart ticking like a bomb (Ma's words, *heart ticking like a bomb*), and her only fourteen years old, and Paps only sixteen, both in the ninth grade, and then both dropping out. Ma had to convince Paps to do the right thing, which was to take her on a bus to Texas and marry her. She told us how she was eight months fat by then, and Paps was dark and Afroed. The two of them were so Brooklyn and baby faced and mixed up that the politest thing people could think to do was stare, and the world is full of people who ain't polite — but it had to be Texas, Ma explained, on account of Ma's being too young to marry in New York. So then they were married, so then came Joel, so then came me. All three born in Ma's teenage years ("my teenage years," Ma repeated, as if that meant something to us) — after we learned about all that, we were no longer Three Billy Goats Gruff crossing the bridge, we were no longer the three trolls that lived under the bridge.

After that, we played a new game where the trolls tricked sex on the goats and we were the babies — half gruff, half troll.

We walked out, all three together, far from the house, to the drugstore. We planted ourselves on the concrete and held out fistfuls of change and asked strangers to buy us troll things — cigarettes or beers or whiskeys — but no one would. They told us to scram, or they said things like "Whiskeys? Shit, y'all are just babies."

"Troll babies!" we screamed. "Gruff babies!"

When a pregnant woman waddled up, Manny shot to his feet, pointing his finger and shouting, "Hey, lady, you got a bomb in there?"

We kicked our sneakers against the concrete and howled. Joel threw the change up in the air, and it rained down silver jingles. We laughed and laughed, saying, "A bomb! Oh God, a bomb!"

The lady didn't walk away; she tilted her head, curious, rubbing her palms slowly all over her belly, waiting for us to calm, before saying, "*This?* This is a baby. This is my baby."

Her eyes were wet, black-hole eyes — no fear there, no disgust, no pity — she was wide open, this lady. She was drinking us in.

When she said "Stand up," we did just that. Same with "Come here."

She squatted a little and took our wrists, one at a time, and placed them on her belly.

"You just gotta wait," she said—but we didn't have to wait for long.

"Hot damn!" said Joel. "It's trying to get out!"

"Does it got a daddy?"

"All babies got daddies."

"He trick you?"

"Trick me?"

"How old are you?"

"Mind your p's and q's."

"You fourteen?"

"Fourteen? God, no."

"Does it hurt?"

"Some. It'll hurt real bad when they take him out."

"It'll hurt your vagina."

"Don't you all know how to be proper?"

We looked at our sneakers. Manny swept up the change from the ground and pressed it into her hand.

"Here," he said, "give this to your baby. Tell him it's from us."

"Us who?"

"Us three."

"Us brothers."

"Us Musketeers."

"Us tricks."

And after that—after we left that lady holding our small fortune and tinkling it around in her palm—we raced home, pulled Ma down onto the sofa, and lifted her shirt, kissing and blowing raspberries onto her belly—so thin and tight now, no room for us — asking, "Us hurt you?" knowing that we had lived there once, in Ma's belly, before we were three together, before we were brothers.

And Ma? She didn't question, she just let herself be pulled down, flat on her back, laughing; she just gave in, our Ma, raising her arms above her head, surrender style; she just gave herself up.

LINA

PAPS DISAPPEARED for a while, and Ma stopped showing up for work, stopped eating, stopped cooking for us, stopped flushing cigarette butts down the toilet, and let them pile up instead, inside of empty bottles and in teacups; wet cigarette butts clogged the drain of the sink. She stopped sleeping in her bed and took to the couch instead, or the floor, or sometimes she slept at the kitchen table, with her head in one arm and the other arm dangling down toward the linoleum, where little heaps of cigarette butts and empty packs and ash piled up around her.

We tiptoed. We ate peanut butter on saltine crackers and angel hair pasta coated in vegetable oil and grated cheese. We ate things from the back of the refrigerator, long-forgotten things, Harry and David orange marmalades, with the rinds floating inside like insects trapped in amber. We ate instant stuffing and white rice with soy sauce or ketchup.

Lina, Ma's supervisor, called to check up.

"This makes six shifts in a row," she said. "What's going on over there?"

Machinery buzzed and clanked around her. There was the piercing clatter of bottles being hustled down an assembly line.

"What do you mean?" I asked.

"Speak up, honey," she hollered. "It's louder than hell where I am."

"What do you mean?"

"I mean it's loud here! I can barely hear you. Fuck it. I guess I'll just have to come over and see for myself." The line went dead, and I waited for the dial tone and then that other noise, the one that means that you've forgotten to hang up the phone.

Lina came straight from the brewery, still in her long white lab coat, her safety goggles perched on top of her head. She was born in China; she was tall and thick, with high cheekbones that stuck out like handlebars below her eyes.

"You're huge," we said. "There's no room for you. You'll bump your head on the ceiling."

We tried to close the door on her, but she muscled it open and held up one of her legs, pointing to her boot.

"I'm shorter without these."

She took off her coat, talking about how there was a part of China where all the women were built like her, "like Cadillacs," she said and laughed, holding out her big hands on either side of her in a motion that was meant to imply hugeness. She handed us a brown paper grocery bag, bent down to unlace her boots, and said, "Don't open that just yet, just set it on the table and fetch me your mother from wherever she's hiding."

"She's sleeping," Manny grunted. We didn't bother taking the groceries into the kitchen. We dumped everything onto the living room carpet and tore into the sliced bread and cheese, jamming fistfuls into our mouths, drinking the milk out of the carton, looking straight into Lina's eyes, the three of us, daring her. She flashed her long, wide horse teeth at us. She tossed her boots into the corner.

"You'll choke," she warned, "if you're not careful.

"Comrade!" she hollered, stepping over us, and Ma came running, throwing herself into Lina's big arms, burying her face in Lina's silky black hair, and crying.

Lina stood there for a while, then reached into her smock and pulled out a tissue, taking our mother's face in her hands and wiping it down, tucking wisps of hair behind Ma's ears. We were kneeling on the floor, not two feet away from them, and the longer Lina stood there, grooming Ma, the less we paid attention to the groceries. Then Lina started kissing Ma all over, little soft kisses, covering Ma's whole face with them, even her nose and eyebrows. Then she put her lips on Ma's lips and held them there, soft and still, and nobody — not me, not Ma, not Joel or Manny, nobody — said a word. There wasn't a word to say.

OTHER LOCUSTS

WE GOT INTO Old Man's garden and helped ourselves. Old Man had a high hedge and lived down a dirt road almost too rough and rutted for our bikes, but we forged the road, pushed through the hedge, got into the garden, and helped ourselves. We tasted and trampled and laid waste, and when we looked up, Old Man was watching us from the porch, just watching.

"Animals," he hissed. He looked as if he could spit. "Locusts."

We were ashamed before him. He was very old.

"This your garden?" Manny asked. Joel let a tomato fall from his hand, then wiped his mouth with the back of his wrist.

Old Man opened the screen door and came down the steps toward us. He dropped to his knees in the dirt and fingered the broken stalks. He picked up a half-eaten cucumber and brushed away the dirt, then flipped open a pocketknife and cleaved away the bite marks. The plants we had pulled up from the roots were pushed back into the earth. He crawled stiffly around on hands and knees, and we stood above watching.

Old Man pushed the salvaged vegetable parts into our arms, then herded us onto the porch. We dumped the pieces onto a fold-out card table.

"What's locusts?" Joel asked.

"What the locust swarm left, the great locusts have eaten; what the great locusts have left, the young locusts have eaten; what the young locusts have left" — Old Man paused to narrow his eyes at each one of us — "other locusts have eaten."

Then he called us invaders, marauders, scavengers, the devil's army on earth.

Old Man spoke crooked and singsong — a Missouri accent, it turned out — and we didn't understand half the words he used, but locusts, the threat and possibility of locusts, seized our imaginations, and we made Old Man tell us about them over and over again until we understood. We even made him draw us a picture of locusts, a flurry of black marker dashes near the top of the page, the sky, more and more dashes, one on top of the other, until the top half of the page was filled with black.

"That there's locusts," he said. "You'll see, by the by, you'll see."

This was all on the porch; he never invited us any farther into his home than that, but neither did he ask us to leave. It was late afternoon, sunset, dusk, into evening; the late summer air cooled quickly but didn't chill. The porch was screened in; the screens had bits of fabric sewn right into their mesh to patch up the holes and keep out the mosquitoes, but the mosquitoes found their way in anyhow. Old Man called them skeeters.

We sat around that fold-out table and slapped them skeeters dead on the tabletop or on each other's exposed calves or forearms — we made a game of it, slapping at each other and laughing, but if a skeeter landed on Old Man, we didn't slap or smack but brushed his dry skin with our fingers. Once I stood and blew a gust of air across the back of Old Man's neck, where a skeeter perched to bite, and Old Man winked and nudged me in the ribs.

"Best medicine for a skeeter bite is to cut a cross, like this," he said and carved a tiny cross onto my arm with his thumbnail. "That way you break up the poison and kill the itch."

Old Man was from the Ozarks, which was a place in Missouri with sinkholes and caves and backward lightning that rose up from the earth and stretched into the sky.

Old Man told us we were on the lam. He had all kinds of names for us, castaways, stowaways, hideaways, fugitives, punks, city slickers, bastards. Manny told him we had run away and weren't ever going back, and Joel added that our mother was dead, so there wasn't nobody to call anyhow. He was very old, and he didn't seem to care to call anyone or do anything. He also called us sweets, babies, innocents, poor pitiful creatures, God's own. He strung the words together, and talked mostly to himself, all the while chopping those vegetables into smaller and smaller pieces on the table; what he was doing was this: making us a salad.

He got up and went into the house to fetch a bowl and plates and forks. He moved very slowly.

"Old Man's all right," said Manny.

"He is too," said Joel.

Joel spotted the yellow of a plastic wiffle-ball bat among some rakes and brooms and shovels, all leaning in a corner.

"What's he got this for?"

He dug out the bat and looked around, but there was no ball. He faked a slow home-run swing, filling his cheeks with air and exhaling the moment he imagined making contact.

"And don't tell lies about Ma being dead," Manny said to Joel. "That shit ain't right."

It had gotten so dark that the light from the porch prevented us from seeing into the yard beyond. Our Ma was still broken, still dead-eyed, but she was not dead. She'd even returned to the brewery. She'd be there now, working. And our Paps was still disappeared. Manny said he'd picked up with another woman.

Joel took another home-run swing, then faked the roaring of a crowd. Soon we would have to walk our bikes home in the dark, down that rutted-up dirt road without any streetlights.

"You hear?"

"You think you know everything," Joel said, pointing

the tip of the bat close to Manny's nose. Manny flared and tensed and Joel smiled. "But you don't know shit."

"The fuck I don't," Manny said, and the words were barely spoken before the bat was swung, snapping Manny's head sideways. Then they were on the ground, fighting in the worst way — kennel style, Paps called it, all teeth and tearing and snot and blood.

I yelled for them to stop, that's all I did, yelled that one word over and over, *stop, stop, stop.* I thought of Ma, whispering that same *stop, stop, stop* to our father. Manny sucked down the snot from his nose into his throat and spat a lugie in Joel's face, and the mucus slid off, like egg yolk.

"Animals," said Old Man, *"animals."*

Then Manny and Joel did stop. They stood and panted and pulled their clothes back into shape. Old Man stayed in the doorway to his house and ordered us off his porch, into all that dark. The air buzzed with insects. There was no moon. Summer nights seemed the wildest nights of all.

There were still millions of questions, about God, and locusts, and the Ozarks, about getting old and dying. Old Man held our bowls in his hand, and because we could not look him in the eye, we looked at those empty bowls. We looked so silently, we looked so hard, that he turned from us and set the bowls down somewhere inside the house.

"Go on," he said, "scram."

Millions of questions. Like, how come animals aren't afraid of the dark? Especially the tiny ones, the bunnies and little birds that are skittish enough during the day — what do they make of the night? How do they understand it? How can they sleep out there, alone? Were the trees and bushes and rabbit holes all filled with ears listening, listening, and eyes never daring to shut?

And the other locusts, what's wrong with them, why do they come last, and what's left for them to eat?

TALK TO ME

W E W E R E S E A T E D at the kitchen table, hungry, impatient, clamoring. We threw our heads back on our necks and grasped our bellies. Every night we died of hunger. Ma was suckling her fingertip; she had cut herself on the jagged edge of the soup can. The phone rang, and Ma spun around and popped the cut finger out of her mouth.

"It's your father," she said but didn't answer, just dumped the soup into the pot and resumed her bloodsucking.

We stopped whining and looked back and forth from each other to the ringing phone — this was a new game. We rested our elbows on the tabletop, held our faces in the palms of our hands, and watched her back, mirroring her silence, waiting for the next move, but she didn't look at us or offer an explanation; she just kept stirring. The phone rang as the soup simmered and hissed, the phone rang as Ma splashed the broth into three bowls and slid them under our faces, the phone rang as we extended our chins and noses into the steam and stuck out our tongues to taste the hot air. We hadn't seen or heard from our father in weeks.

Ma ripped open a bag of crackers, scattered them across a plate, clattered that plate onto the middle of the table, and said, "What? Eat."

She joined us, her chair turned sideways. She unlaced her work boots, slipped off her socks, and massaged her feet. The phone rang just above and behind her head. She knew where Paps was at, knew the secret of his urgency, and she wasn't going to tell us. The foot massage was a bad sign, but worse was the smile when we asked for more dinner.

"That's it," she said, smiling her crooked tooth smile, staring at her painted toenails. "That's all there is."

We stayed at the table for another forty-five minutes, running our fingers around our empty bowls, pressing our thumb tips into the cracker plate and licking the crumbs off, lulled into a trance by the even tempo of the phone's ring, immobilized by the repetition, listening carefully, hoping it would never stop. He was somewhere, at some phone, in a phone booth, or sitting on the edge of a someone else's bed, drunk or sober, and it was loud and hot, or cold, and he was alone, or there were others, but every single ring brought him home, brought him right there before us. The tone of the ringing changed too, from desperate to accusatory to something sad and slow, then it was a heartbeat, then it was eternity — had always rung, would always ring — then it was the piercing bell of an alarm.

Ma stood up from her chair, lifted the receiver, and

placed it back down again in one swift movement — and for a moment nothing, maybe even a full minute, long enough for our ears and clenched muscles to relax, long enough to remember and realize fully something we had long suspected: that silence was absolution, that quiet was as close to happiness as we would ever get. But then it started again, the ringing, and continued.

"What if he's having a heart attack?" Manny asked.

"What heart?" said Ma.

"I'm going to get it," Manny said, and without even a second's hesitation our mother grabbed his bowl and smashed it onto the linoleum.

And still the phone rang.

Ma dismissed us, and Manny went and shut himself up in our room, so Joel and I headed down to the crawlspace, where we sharpened popsicle sticks into points, preparing for war. Footsteps were amplified in the crawlspace, voices muffled, and the phone didn't exist at all.

Paps finally arrived home, and they made thunder, stomping above us, chasing each other, tumbling furniture. Their screams and curses reached us not as words but as soft, blunt rhythms. One of them finally got in the car and left, then nothing, silence, except for the light scraping of a broom.

We climbed farther back in the crawlspace, as far as we could go, to the cinderblock wall. We found a heap of relics, a patchwork purse with fake, crackling leather, a broken typewriter, and our old yellow phone. Joel spun the dial.

"Ring ring," he said.

I used my thumb to hear and my pinky to speak.

"Hello?"

"Mami, how come you don't answer the phone when I call you?"

"'Cause you sound so ugly!" I said, and we bust up laughing.

I grabbed the phone and called him.

"Yo, yo, whassup."

"Woman, this is your husband talking to you right now, you better act right."

"What do you want from me?"

I stared at the receiver in my hand; I couldn't think of anything to say, so Joel took the phone and called me instead.

"Hello?"

"*Dígame*, Mami," he said. "Talk to me."

"I been missing you, at work, them long-ass hours, I been missing you real bad."

"I know, Mami, I know."

We both hung up; we weren't really laughing anymore, weren't really looking at each other, but we were smiling. After a pause, Joel called me.

"Hello?"

"I got a job!"

"You got a *job?*"

"Yeah, baby, everything's going to be real fine from now on, just real fine."

We both hung up, but I called him back right away.

"I'm sorry."

"Nah, baby," Joel said. "I'm sorry."

The next time Joel called me, I made my voice sexy.

"Hey, you," I said.

"Hey yourself," he said, and we both hung up, blushing.

I called Joel.

"Hello?"

"What are we gonna do?"

"What do you mean, 'What are we gonna do?'"

"It's just going to be like this forever?"

"No, baby, it's not going to be like this forever."

"So what are we going to do?"

"Well, we'll do whatever it takes, I guess," Joel said.

I was confused about who he was pretending to be.

"What does it take?"

"I'm not sure yet." He stretched the cord like a bow and arrow, then let it fly.

YOU BETTER COME

NOW THAT PAPS had returned, he wanted to be with us, all five together, all the time. He herded us into the kitchen and gave us big knives to chop up the onions and cilantro while he picked through the dried beans and boiled the rice and Ma chatted at him and smelled the air and sent us winks.

After dinner he led us all to the bathtub, no bubbles, just six inches of gray water and our bare butts, our knees and elbows, and our three little dicks. Paps scrubbed us rough with a soapy washcloth. He dug his fingernails into our scalp as he washed our hair and warned us that if the shampoo got into our eyes, it was our own fault for squirming. We made motorboat noises, navigating bits of Styrofoam around toothpicks and plastic milk-cap islands, and we tried to be brave when he grabbed us; we tried not to flinch.

Ma was leaning over the sink, peering into the mirror, pulling out her eyebrows and curling her eyelashes with shiny metal instruments. "Be gentle," she said without even looking at him, without even blinking her eyes.

They were both topless; Ma was in a flesh-colored bra and heavy cotton work pants, and Paps had taken off his shirt to wash us. We saw everything — how our skin was darker than Ma's but lighter than Paps's, how Ma was slight and nimble, with ribs softly stepping down from her breasts, how Paps was muscled, the muscles and tendons of his forearms, the veins in his hands, the kinky hairs spreading across his chest. He was like an animal, our father, ruddy and physical and instinctive; his shoulders hulked and curved, and we had, each of us, even Ma, sat on them, gone for rides. Ma's shoulders were clipped, slipping away from her tiny bird neck. She was just over five feet and light enough for Manny to lift, and when Paps called her fragile, he sometimes meant for us to take extra-special care with her, and he sometimes meant that she was easily broken.

Paps stood to piss and we saw his stout, fleshy dick, the darkness of his skin down there and the strong jet of urine, long and loud and pungent. Ma turned from the mirror; we saw her watching him too. He zipped up and stood behind her, then slid his hands under her bra, and mounds of flesh rolled and squished between his fingers. It made us giddy because it made her giddy, even though she pushed him away. They were playing with each other, and no one wanted to leave the bathroom, no one wanted to fight or splash or ruin the moment.

Paps leaned against the wall and watched her adjusting herself back into her harness; he grinned and he growled. We watched him watching her, we studied his hunger, and he knew we were seeing and understanding. Now he winked at us; he wanted us to know that she made him happy.

"That's my girl," he said, slapping her bottom. "Ain't another one like her."

"They're going to catch pneumonia," Ma said, so he fished us out of the tub, one at a time, and stood us on the toilet seat and toweled us dry. He grabbed our ankles and dried the undersides of our feet, and we had to hold on to his shoulder for balance or grab a fistful of his Afro. He ran the towel between our toes, our butt cracks, our armpits, tickling us, but acting as if he couldn't comprehend what was so ticklish. He dried our heads for a long time, until we were smarting and dizzy.

Each time Paps finished drying one of us, he would place our palm against his own palm. He didn't say anything to Joel or Manny, but my hand he held up a little longer, looking close and nodding his head.

"You grew," he said, and I smiled and straightened my back, broadening my shoulders, triumphant.

Ma and Paps started talking to each other about our bodies, about how quickly we were changing; they joked about needing to make some more boys to take our places. We watched them; they looked each other in the eyes, teasing and laughing; their words were warm and soft, and we snuggled into the gentleness of their conversation. We were all together in the bathroom, in this moment, and nothing was wrong. My brothers and I were clean and fed and not afraid of growing up.

We climbed back into the empty tub, still in our towels, and our parents pretended not to notice. We saw them pretending and it thrilled us. We slid the shower curtain closed and huddled together, looking at each other with wide-open, eager eyes.

"Hey, wait a minute," Paps said in mock surprise, "where did the boys go?"

We pressed our fists into our cheeks to keep back the giggles.

"Oh my," Ma said. "They just disappeared."

We clenched ourselves together into a tighter ball. Our knees tensed with excitement. They were going to find us. Maybe they'd scare us, yanking back the curtain and shouting "Gotcha!" Maybe they'd scoop us up and tickle us; maybe they'd be sneaky and stand on the rim of the tub and peek over the top of the curtain, waiting for us to notice. Maybe they'd roar like dinosaurs; maybe they'd devour us. Maybe Paps would take Joel under one arm and Manny under the other, and maybe Ma would grab me and swing me in a circle, but whatever happened, we would be found, my brothers and me, huddled together; they would grab us and take us up and into their arms and own us.

But then they didn't look for us at all; they found each other instead. We listened to their kissing and soft little moans, and after a while we got down on our knees, lifting up the bottom edge of the shower curtain and spying on them. Ma was balanced on the sink, her back to the mirror and her legs folded around Paps's waist. She dragged her fingers up and down his back. Her hands were little and light, with painted fingernails that traced ridges into Paps's skin.

Paps's hands seemed massive on her tiny frame. He clutched her hips, moving her toward and then away from him, steadily, stealthily, squeezing hard enough so that his fingers appeared to be sinking into her sides like into quicksand, and when I looked at her face she looked like she was in pain, but she didn't look frightened, like it was a kind of pain she wanted.

We saw everything — that Paps's blue jeans were faded in the spot where he kept his wallet, the muscles of his stomach, that Ma closed her eyes but Paps kept his open, that he bit, that they were both gripping tight, that Ma's ankles were crossed and her toes were pointed. Her legs clutched and released him, and he was leaning her back so that her skin touched the skin of her reflection, like a picture I once saw of Siamese twins. The faucet poked into the base of her spine, and it must have hurt her, all of it must have hurt her, because Paps was much bigger and heftier, and he was rough with her, just like he was rough with us. We saw that it must hurt her, too, to love him.

Paps leaned Ma all the way back, her hair mixing and reflecting, doubling itself in the mirror. He bit into her neck like an apple, and she rolled her head over and spotted us. She smiled. She pulled Paps's head away from her and turned him until he spotted us too.

"I thought you disappeared," he said.

"You were supposed to look for us," said Manny.

"I guess I found something better," Paps said, and Ma slapped him on the chest and called him a bastard. She unwrapped herself from him and fidgeted with her clothes and smoothed her hair. He tried to kiss her neck again, but she wiggled away.

"Get my boots from the closet," she said. "Please, Papi, I'm already late."

We sighed and sank onto our butts, but the moment Paps left the bathroom, Ma turned off the light and shut the door and got into the tub with us, pulling the curtain closed behind her. It was completely dark; we couldn't even see her, but we could feel her arms around us, her hair tickling my bare shoulders.

"We'll show him," Ma said, and we loved her then, fiercely.

We heard him clomp up the stairs. We got ready to pounce. Then his hand was on the doorknob, he paused, and for a second it seemed as if he might have figured us out, but he came in and flicked on the light, and we rushed out from behind the curtain, tackling him into the hallway and onto the floor. Ma sat on his chest and we tickled him everywhere. He laughed a throaty all-out laugh, kicking his legs, saying "No! No! No!" — laughing and laughing until he was wheezing and there were tears in his eyes — but even then we kept on tickling, poking our fingers into his sides and tickling his feet, all of us laughing and making as much noise as we could, but no one as loud as Paps.

"No! No! No!" he said, crying now, laughing still. "I can't breathe!"

"All right," Ma said, "that's enough."

But it was not enough. Our towels had slipped off, and blood pumped through our naked bodies, our hands shook with energy, we were alive and it was not enough; we wanted more. We started tickling Ma too, started poking her, and she collapsed onto Paps's chest and covered her head, and he wrapped his arms around her.

Then Manny slapped Ma hard on the back. It sounded so satisfying, the thwack of his palm on her skin.

"You were supposed to come find us," he said.

Joel and I froze, waiting for some sign of trouble, waiting for Paps to react, threaten him, hit him, something. We stood there, hunched and alert like startled cats, but nothing came. Manny slapped her back again, and still nothing. Silence. Ma only moved both her hands to Paps's wrists. Her hair covered their faces, and we understood that we could do this, that this would be allowed, and never spoken of.

Joel kicked Paps's thigh as hard as he could.

"Yeah," he said, "you're supposed to find us."

I joined in, kicking for Paps but hitting Ma; it felt dull and mean and perfect. Then we were all three kicking and slapping at once, and they didn't say a word, they didn't even move; the only noise was the noise of skin and impact and breath, and then our protests, *why don't you come find us, why don't you do what you're supposed to do, come and find us, why don't ya, because you're bad, bad, bad, bad, bad, why don't you do right, why can't you do right, we hate you, come and find us, we hate you, everyone hates you, you better come and find us, next time, next time you better come.*

We hit and we kept on hitting; we were allowed to be what we were, frightened and vengeful — little animals, clawing at what we needed.

NIGHT WATCH

PAPS FOUND A NIGHT job, and since Ma still worked
graveyards at the brewery, where there was no place to
hide little boys, weeknights we went to work with Paps and
slept on the floor, in front of the vending machines. Paps
was the security guard, the night watch.

One night I woke sweating and twisted inside my sleeping bag. I kicked free and stood looking down on my
brothers, their faces painted orange from the light coming
through the window, and their shadowed jack-o'-lantern
eyes. I walked over to the desk where Paps sat watching a
little television monitor, leaning back in his chair, holding
both cigarette and beer bottle slack-armed and low to the
floor.

I asked if it was almost time to go home.

Paps did his dog growl, he snapped his teeth, but then
he set his bottle down and pulled me onto his lap anyway. I
rested my face against his chest, and he ran his hand down

along my spine from the base of my skull to my lower back; he kept doing that.

"I like sleeping in a bed," I said.

"Me too," Paps said. "Me too."

From his lap, I could see outside the window. A few feet away, on the brick wall of the next building, a single orange bulb was locked inside a metal mesh box.

"Why is that light in a cage?" I asked.

"Same reason you cage a bird," Paps said.

"What's that mean?"

"So it don't fly away."

"Can you unlock it?"

"What do you think?"

After some time, Paps shut the little TV on the desk.

"I think the noise woke you up," he whispered close to my ear, and I nodded approvingly. I could feel the muscles in his chest, and underneath, his heart working. I fell asleep.

The next time I woke, I was still in Paps's arms, but he was shaking me awake and setting me down and saying, "Fuck. Fuck. Fuck."

He stepped over to where Manny and Joel were sleeping and prodded them with the tip of his boot.

"Up," he said. "Hurry."

My brothers groaned and tried to roll away from him.

"Get a move on," Paps hollered. "We're late!"

Before they were even fully standing, Paps was already on his knees gathering up the bedding, yanking so wildly that Joel got tangled and fell back down. We busted up laughing until Paps smacked Manny openhanded across the face and Manny yelped; then we were silent.

"Take your brothers out to the car and get under the covers and stay there until I come out." He shook Manny back and forth by one arm. *"Entiendes?"*

When we got outside, the morning man was there, Paps's replacement — taller than Paps, and white. He blew into a Styrofoam cup, and the cup billowed its own steam back at him. When he spotted the three of us, he stopped blowing and set the cup on a low wall that separated the sidewalk from the building's narrow yard.

Left to right, right to left, his gaze, cold and curious, touched down on each of our faces, our heaps of blankets, even our little rubber snow boots. No one spoke; only Manny shifted slightly to cover his cheek with a blanket. Then Paps came out and broke the spell, pushing past us on the stairs and extending his hand to the other man, shaking it once and firm, saying "Morning" loud and direct in his face.

"These yours?"

"That's what she keeps telling me."

The man lowered himself to his haunches. He frowned.

"Well, at least you're only half as ugly looking as your Daddy is."

We were half as ugly, half as dark, half as wild. Adults were always leaning in and explaining that we must have inherited this from Ma and that from Paps. We all three kept our eyes above the man, on Paps, who was still standing. He flashed us a look that was impossible to interpret, but serious, so serious.

"What's all this?" the man asked, tugging at a corner of my sleeping bag.

I looked at Joel standing next to me; Joel looked at Manny.

"Listen, man," Paps said. "Let's you and I have a talk."

"Your Daddy got you sleeping on the floor?"

"I said let's you and I have a talk."

The man rose up to his full height.

"Talk?"

Paps reached in his pocket, pulled out the car keys, and rested them on top of Manny's bundle. "Get your brothers settled in the car," he said quietly, "and don't drop anything."

Turning back to the man, Paps said, "What? You can talk to my kids, but not to me?"

In the car, we squished into the front, kneeling on the passenger seat, leaning our elbows on the dashboard, and cupping our faces in our hands. We peered out the windshield to the steps, where Paps and the other man smoked and gestured back and forth, Paps aiming a finger at the man, or at us in the car, or up at the sky, and the man mostly holding his hands, palms out, up by his chest and pushing the air away from him. Steam and smoke rose from their mouths, and the coffee cup sat untouched on the low wall.

"How much you wanna bet Paps slugs him?" Manny asked.

"Look at that man," Joel said. "That man don't want a fight."

"He fell asleep," I said.

"Who?"

"Paps. He fell asleep."

Joel and Manny quit jostling for the best position and studied Paps more closely.

"So it's not our fault?" Joel asked.

"Some," Manny said. "Some's always ours."

Paps walked over to the man's coffee cup and smacked it, swinging wild, like he was trying to fly it out of the lot. We watched the brown liquid jump up in an arc and splatter on the pavement. The man narrowed his eyes at Paps, shook his head, and spat on the ground, walking away from him, into the building.

By the time Paps opened the car door, Manny and Joel had already hustled into the back and buckled up, trying to shrink to invisible, but Paps turned in his seat, grabbed hold of Manny's hair, and said, "Keys!"

Manny handed him the keys.

"When I say move, you move, you understand me?"

No one said anything.

He let go of Manny and turned to me, gripping my chin and digging his fingers into my cheek. "Understand me?"

"Yes, sir."

We drove home in silence, each one of us sliding fingers into the condensation on our windows. Close to home, Manny had the nerve to ask, "You gonna get fired?"

Paps laughed — one quick, nasty bark of a laugh.

Manny tried again.

"What'd that man say to you anyway?"

"What do you think?"

Paps punched the ceiling. The noise jolted us to attention, and we braced ourselves for worse, but nothing followed.

"Man, that's what he always says — 'What do you think?'" Manny said in a too-loud mocking voice, but Paps didn't seem to hear; he just drove.

"Yeah," I said. "That's what he said last night. About the light."

"What light?"

"The light in the cage outside the window. I asked if he could unlock it, and he said, 'What do you think?'"

Joel considered this like a real thinker, one hand tucked up in his armpit and the other pinching his chin. "What *do* you think?" he asked.

"That's not the point," Manny said.

"I bet he could unlock it," Joel said to the two of us. Grabbing the back of his seat and leaning forward, he said to Paps, "I bet you could unlock that light. Couldn't you?"

Paps cleared his throat and swallowed hard, but he didn't speak.

"Sure he could," I said, leaning in with Joel. "Sure you could, Paps, couldn't you?"

"Course he could," said Manny, joining us. "Nobody's saying you couldn't unlock it, Paps. Nobody's saying *that*."

Paps started making odd, wheezy, gasping noises. He slammed the dashboard with his palm, then closed his fist and really started thumping with force, but slow and steady, as if he was beating down a nail. Eventually, he fell into a three-beat rhythm, more like beating a drum, keeping time to some music only he heard. He wiped snot from his nose and water from his eyes, but went on pounding. Thump. Thump. Thump.

"He crying?" Joel whispered.

"What, with his fist?"

It didn't seem much like crying, seemed like something else, meaner than crying; steadier, too, but not one of us had ever actually seen him cry, so we couldn't know for sure — and Paps, he didn't say a word about it, just the thump, thump, thump, for miles. When we thought he would stop, he didn't; when we thought he would speak or scream or cuss, he was silent. His breathing calmed some, but the water and snot kept coming, and the wheeze, and the gasp.

After a while the pounding, so spooky at first, was just there, and a while after that, Joel started smacking his own fist against the window, in time with Paps.

Thump. Thump. Thump.

Then it was Manny against his window, matching the beat. Paps didn't turn back or acknowledge us at all; he just kept up his pounding, so I pounded on the hard plastic armrest in the middle, and it felt like we were building something, a tribe — us four together, us four angry and giddy and thump-crazy, together.

Once we turned onto our street, we tried out little three-word chants to the beat of our pounding.

"No More Work!" said Manny.

"No More Floor!" I said.

"No! More! Coffee Cups!" yelled Joel, and we all bust up laughing; even Paps spat out a little laugh of surprise.

We rolled all over the back seat, slapping our thighs, trying to chant "No More Coffee Cups" but choking on the words, we were laughing so hard, until Manny said, "Stop, stop. I can't anymore. I'm crying."

Joel responded by pounding out "No More Crying!" on the window. And soon we were all pounding it out.

"No More Crying! No More Crying!"

All the way down the street and into the driveway, we chanted, up the front steps and into the house, where Ma had already arrived and undressed for sleep and came now to the bedroom door in her bra and underwear, rubbing her eyes, asking what in hell was going on; we chanted and pounded the walls, we pounded the coffee table in front of the couch, where Paps had slumped and covered his eyes with the palms of his hands. "No More Crying! No More Crying!"

Ma tried to holler over the noise; she kept asking what in hell was going on, calling on Paps by his first name to tell her what in hell was going on, sitting by him, putting the back of her hand to his forehead, and then to us saying, "He's just tired, he's just tired is all," and then looking at him, "You're just tired, baby, aren't you?"

Paps kept his palms over his eyes; he spoke like that.

"We're never gonna escape this," Paps said. "Never."

We didn't know who he was talking to, but it hushed us. Our thumps softened to taps against the tabletop; we still chanted, but it was almost a whisper now and no fun.

"You talking about escaping?" Ma asked.

"Nobody," Paps said. "Not us. Not them. Nobody's ever escaping this." He raised his head and swept his arm out in front of him. *"This."*

Finally, we were silent.

Ma stood and grabbed his outstretched hand with both of hers and pulled it down and buried it in the space between them.

"Don't," she said in a voice more steady than we knew. "Don't you dare."

BIG-DICK TRUCK

PAPS DROVE OFF to the car dealership, and the three of us staked out in the front lawn all afternoon, snapping the yellow dandelion heads off their stems and streaking them down our arms, painting ourselves in gold, waiting for him to return.

Our old car had died the night before, on the way back home, after dropping Ma off at work. The engine just quit, right in the middle of the highway, in the rain. Paps had punched and punched the wheel, his fist cry, cursing in English, then Spanish, then just dropping his head into his hands, saying nothing for a long time, rubbing his eyes with his palms, breathing deep. After a while, he fished around and found some plastic shopping bags on the floor of the car. He tied the bags around our heads, and we all got out, very carefully, and walked down the shoulder, soaking up the spray from the tractor-trailers, until finally someone, a woman, pulled over and gave us a ride.

Once we were inside the woman's car and Paps had

thanked her a few times, he turned in his seat and said to us, "Tomorrow. Tomorrow I am going to the dealership, and we're getting a new car."

We didn't believe him, but the woman did; she thought it was a wonderful idea, and she stretched her neck and peered into the rearview mirror, trying to catch our expression.

But then in the morning, Ma agreed: we *were* getting a new car, today.

Now we were in the front yard, waiting, Manny with a pair of plastic binoculars and Joel up in a tree, lying about how he could see all the way to the dealership. A pickup truck turned the corner, and Manny whispered, "It's him." He said it so softly and clearly that we knew he wasn't jerking us, and we took off running down the block, pulling on each other's sleeves, stumbling, slaphappy.

When Paps saw us coming, he started celebrating, hooting and hollering, but he had the windows rolled up, so we couldn't hear anything he was saying; we just watched the veins in his neck bulge and his mouth flap open and shut like a puppet. He slowed to a crawl and rolled down the window, and we jogged alongside.

"Well, boys," he said, "meet the newest member of your family."

"No way!" we screamed. Some of the neighborhood kids came out to join us. Our father continued to inch toward the house at his snail's pace, a proud smile on his face, and us kids surrounded the truck, jumping up to try to get a look at the interior, like badly trained dogs.

By the time Paps killed the engine and slid out of the door and onto the gravel driveway, there were at least half a dozen kids examining the truck, climbing into the bed, opening up the glove compartment, running their hands along the leather.

The truck was cobalt blue, with a bench seat and a skinny, two-foot-long gearshift that came up from the floor. Everything was sleek and new, the thick black rubber of the tires and the sparkling chrome of the bumper. The massive side mirrors jutted outward like elephant ears. There were seven other trucks on our block, and ours was the meanest. Immediately, my brothers and I started bossing the other kids around. "Don't be putting your greasy fingers on the glass," we said. "Only us boys can sit in the driver's seat."

Ma came out and stood on the stoop, looking tired and pissed. Her eyes were red and her mouth was set, puckering in on itself. She held her boots in one hand, then let them drop in front of her and sat down on the first step.

"Well, Mami?" Paps asked.

"How many seats does it have?" she said, picking up a boot and jerking at the laces.

"It's a truck," Paps mumbled. "It don't got seats, it got a bench."

Ma smiled at the boot, a mean smile; she didn't look up or look at anything besides that boot. "How many seat belts?"

The neighborhood kids started to climb down and sneak away, all the excitement receding with them like a tide.

"Why you gotta be like that?"

"Me?" Ma said, then she repeated the question, "Me? Me? *Me?*" Each *me* was louder and more frantic than the last. "How many fucking kids do you have? How many fucking kids, and a wife, and how much money do you make? How much do you earn, sitting on your ass all day, to pay for this truck? This fucking truck that doesn't even have enough seat belts to protect your family." She spat in the direction of the driveway. "This fucking big-dick truck."

With that, Paps took one long step toward her and slapped her across the side of her head, but she kept screaming right at him, right up in his face, "Big-dick truck! Big-dick truck!" Her neck and cheeks were flushed red, and she was lost in tears, in rage, shaking her hair loose from her ponytail, pounding Paps on the chest, until finally he clamped a hand across her mouth and pulled her to him with his free arm, pulled her snug up against him and said, "Shush, Mami. Shush."

She struggled and groaned against his grip, until he started saying, "OK. You win," repeating everything a million times. "You win, you win, you win. I'm here, I hear you, you win," and eventually Ma wore herself out, stopped pulling against him, and her face calmed, one hand massaging the spot where she'd been hit.

My brothers and I exchanged disappointed glances; we wanted the truck.

"If she doesn't fit," Manny said, "she doesn't have to ride in it."

Paps shot us a narrow-eyed, watch-it look.

"I'm bringing the truck back tomorrow," he announced, holding Ma a little apart from him so he could look into her eyes. "I'll get a fucking minivan if you want, Mami. I'll get you a fat-lady car, is that what you want, to be a fat old lady?"

We all laughed. Even Ma smiled.

"But tonight we have a truck, so tonight we'll go for a ride, all right?" he asked. "We'll make it a ride we'll never forget, and after, we'll always talk about the time we had a truck for a day."

Ma didn't agree right away, but after dinner she went into the bedroom and came back out in her red dress and her gold hoop earrings, and my brothers and I got our plastic guns from the garage and hopped into the back. We didn't have anywhere to go in particular, so we just drove, cutting through the night, smooth as nothing. We drove through the neighborhood, then out of it, down back roads, past cornfields, Ma in the front, nestled up close to Paps, her head on his shoulder, the wind tossing her hair around both of them, and us boys bumping along in the back, aiming our guns up at the stars above and shooting them down, one by one.

DUCKS

PAPS CAME HOME WITH sleepy eyes and blood-
flushed ears and started leaning against Ma, pressing
her into the counter, kissing her, pinching her in different
places, and Ma, who had been about to leave for the brewery, said, "Stop, stop, stop."

But he didn't stop; he wrapped his arms around her
waist and pulled her toward the bedroom. She dragged
her feet, tried to hold on to the counter, the wall, the door
frame, saying, "Stop, baby, I'm serious," her voice lower-
ing, deepening. "Stop." He lifted her feet off the ground and
pulled her up the stairs, laughing at her anger. She gripped
the banister, and he tugged at her from behind until she let
go. He couldn't see her expression, but we could. Her eyes
searched, wild and desperate, for something to grab, and
for just an instant she looked at us with that same plead-
ing look — she looked to us for help, but we stood there, out
of her reach, watching. Then her face flattened and calmed

some; she even smiled a sad, halfway smile. What did we see there? Disappointment? Forgiveness? All of this passed in a moment, and only a moment, before Paps kicked the door shut.

We boys pulled the blankets from our beds and the cushions from the sofa and made a nest in front of the television. We would not sleep upstairs. We fell asleep with the flash of blue across our eyelids and the moans and whispers of late-night advertisements filling our dreams.

Ma eventually left, worked her graveyard shift, and came home again. She shook us awake, saying, "Get yourselves in that truck, and don't question me. I won't be questioned."

Ma called it that truck, or your father's truck; Paps had never returned the truck like he had promised, and we knew he never would.

We drove out to a park where there was a stepped white gazebo and upside-down canoes half submerged in the river. There were swings with black rubber seats, most of them broken and dangling from their chains into the dirt ruts below. There was a wide and patchy lawn sloping up from the water to the road, and there was our truck parked half on the grass and half on the shoulder. There were no children; all the children were in school.

Inside the bed of the truck were garbage bags stuffed tight with our clothing, the white plastic stretched to a milky translucence and here and there ripped through by the angled edges of letters and envelopes and pictures. Inside the cab was Ma, who had lain across the bench seat and said she needed a nap, pulling her forearm across her eyes to block out the bright day — and all across the lawn was the dew, breaking the sun into specks of light, like a million baby suns clinging to the grass.

The three of us boys trampled around the park, keeping one eye on the truck. We found a sapling bordered by a chicken-wire fence, and we bent the tree to the ground until it snapped into shreds near the base of the trunk — the yellow flesh was moist inside the bark, and sad. Two of us ganged up on the other, then one suddenly switched allegiance and a new brother was bullied and ostracized, then another betrayal, another. We spent the long hours of morning and early afternoon this way, talking nothing but dares and putdowns, saying "Oh, *yeah?*" and cursing. We didn't talk about what might happen next; we were tough guys, and brave.

On the seesaw, Joel held me hostage in the air.

"Let me go," I said.

"Girl, I ain't never gonna let you go," said Joel — but then he did. He jumped off and sent me crashing. My tailbone bucked and vibrated and tried to explode. Still, I got on again, saying, "Promise you won't do it this time?"

And he promised.

And again.

And again.

We made our way along the river's edge, pushing

through the brambles. There was a spot up ahead where the highway bridged the water, and we decided to climb the embankment. The dirt was loose and steep, and there wasn't much to grab on to, but we made our way up, me in the middle, getting pushed from behind by Joel and pulled by Manny once he made it to the top. We walked on the side of the big four-lane road, single file, halfway across the bridge, then we sat so that our feet dangled over the edge and our arms rested on the guardrail. We could feel the air on the back of our necks as the cars whizzed and hummed past. People honked and yelled out of windows to get off the road, and one lady pulled over into the weeds on the other side of the overpass, hollering that this was no place for little boys to sit. We ignored her, but she walked shakily over and offered to drive us wherever we needed to be. We refused politely, looking down at our feet, but she kept insisting that she could not, in good conscience, leave us there, until finally Manny stood and said, "Listen, bitch," and picked up a chunk of pavement, and then Joel and I followed suit, saying "Bitchy-bitch," picking up whatever debris we could find. The lady walked backward to her van.

After we got back to the park and checked to see that Ma was still sleeping in the truck, Joel asked, "The fuck we doing here?" But the question barely registered, spoken, as it was, so softly, and stupid to ask in the first place.

We tipped a canoe upright, tied it to a tree, and climbed in. We fell asleep listening to the soft lap of the water and feeling the dull push of the afternoon sun on our faces. We woke later to the tap of pretzels hitting the fiberglass bottom of the canoe and plunking into the river around us. The sun was gone and the sky was bleeding pink. Ducks paddled over and silently picked the pretzel bits out of the water. Ma, on a bench, smiled at us and laughed.

"I thought you were kidnapped!" she yelled, digging in her purse and tossing more pretzels our way. We flapped our elbows and quacked, and she tried to land the pretzels in our mouths, but she was no good at feeding us.

"Onward!" Ma said, and we followed her back to the truck, clattering on about our day, tattling on each other for all the mean things that had been said and fighting over who got to sit near the window. We peeked into her purse; it was half full with beer pretzels, and we asked where she got them from.

"Your mother," she said, "is a pretty crafty woman."

It was odd to hear her say *your mother,* and for a while I allowed myself to believe that we had a different mother, who tried to help Ma, who filled Ma's purse with snacks.

In the truck, not moving, the four of us crunched the pretzels into dry wads, forcing them down even after our mouths had dried. It was the only food we'd had all day.

"Spain," Ma said, "I've always wanted to go to Spain. We could do that."

I was pretty sure you couldn't drive to Spain, but I couldn't be positive, so when Ma talked about the bullfights and how all the kids would look like us, with brown curls, tan and skinny, and when she talked about cobblestone streets and the life we would build selling bread from wicker baskets in the market, I thought anything was possible. We listened, adding what we could, and made a life.

Dusk settled down, we hadn't driven anywhere, all the lights were off in the truck, and darkness deepened the spaces between us. Ma talked and talked about Spain; she came up with a name for the little dog we would adopt, a dog that would follow us home from school, because in Spain dogs were everywhere, nipping at ankles and begging for crumbs.

On the street, the lampposts blinked on their orange bulbs. The green numbers of the digital clock came to life. A car passed now and then, but overall it was a very quiet road and then suddenly very dark. The lampposts were T-shaped, and they loomed like palm trees, and the circles of light they projected were like small lonesome islands.

The sea of dark reminded me of something Paps was always saying, "Easier to sink than swim." He loved saying that.

The talk slowed, and there were pauses when each of us detached from the others; maybe we were thinking about food or trying to figure out if we were afraid, and if we were, then what we were afraid of, or maybe we were thinking about Paps. Ma tried to keep talking, tried to keep all of it — the silence and hunger and the idea of Paps — at bay, but she was running out of words.

"Honestly," she finally asked, "what should we do?"

She waited.

"We can go home, but we don't have to. We don't ever have to go home again. We can leave him. We can do that. But I need you to tell me what to do."

No one spoke. I tried to listen to faraway noises and guess what they were — animals, satellites. The up-close noises were easy, Ma choking on words, the croak in her throat, the controlled breathing of my brothers.

"Jesus!" Ma whispered. "Say something! You think this is easy?"

"Something," Joel said, and Manny reached across the seat and punched him.

Ma flipped the ignition, and the engine jumped to life. We drove back the way we came, and eventually we pulled into the driveway, home again. We had been terrified she might actually take us away from him this time but also thrilled with the wild possibility of change. Now, at the sight of our house, when it was safe to feel let down, we did. I could feel the bitterness in my brothers' silence; I wondered if Ma felt it too.

"I bet you're hungry," she said. We wouldn't allow ourselves to answer her; we wouldn't allow ourselves to be hungry.

Without another word, she got out and went around to the back to get our bags. A lamp was on in the living room, but the shades were drawn. Ma slammed the door of the truck bed and Paps appeared in the window, parting the curtains and cupping his hand over his eyes and leaning against the glass. The light inside the house was warm and fell around Paps and spilled outside onto the grass, and when Ma opened the door she disappeared in light.

We boys stayed in the truck a bit longer, then we got out and walked away from the house, into the street.

"I thought something was actually going to happen," Joel said. "I thought we were *going* somewhere."

"We should have killed that fucking woman," said Manny. "Taken her keys and driven off."

"Which woman?" I asked, but no one answered me.

"Hell yeah," Joel said. "We should have smashed her fucking skull open. We should have scooped out her brain and fed pieces to the ducks."

"Which woman?"

"Will you listen to this baby?" Joel said to Manny. "*Which woman?* We only seen two women all day, that woman on the bridge and Ma. Unless he's counting himself."

Manny laughed. "It don't matter who, the point's the same. Them ducks wouldn't eat no brains."

"Sure they would. Why not, if they were hungry enough?"

I tried not to listen. I wondered if someone would come along and bandage the tree we had snapped, a park ranger or some kind of doctor who knew about veins and roots, someone who could put it back together.

"They'd get sick. They'd die."

"Did you look at them nasty things? Looked like some hungry-ass ducks to me."

Manny stopped at the lamppost, turned to square off. He had his arms crossed and his head cocked to one side — so Joel crossed his own arms and cocked his head right back.

"I'm telling you," Manny said, "them ducks are too smart to eat them bitches' brains."

TRENCH

W E WOKE TO THE sound of Paps digging out
back, his grunt, his heave, his shovel hack. We
pushed open the upstairs window and leaned out into the
early morning sky, sleepy and confused, still in our underwear, our skin one shade of deep summer brown. If Paps
had looked up, we would have appeared to him like a three-
torsoed beast, but he didn't look up, and we didn't call down
to him.

For the past few weeks we had been dressing in oversize
camouflage from a box of hand-me-downs Ma had brought
home from work. Someone had died, someone army. We
cut the sleeves and the length from the shirts; we wore cargo
shorts as pants. We fastened everything with green canvas
belts and sliding army buckles. There were caps and bandan-
nas and exactly three olive-mesh tank tops that shrank in
on themselves and were meant to be worn tight but draped
on us, the shoulder holes opening down to our waists. The
mesh shirts were our favorite, like wearing nothing at all.

Manny smeared a thumb's worth of shoe polish under our eyes, then we stepped out quietly through the door and crept along the side of the house, slipping underneath a hedge, army spies. For the past few weeks, we had been at war.

"He's digging a grave," whispered Joel.

"Whose grave?" I asked.

"Nah," whispered Manny, "that there's a trench."

"That ain't no trench," Joel replied. "That's a grave."

"But whose grave?"

"How am I supposed to know? Ma's grave, I guess. Maybe it's your grave."

"No way," I said. "No way that's my grave."

Paps kept digging and digging, shovels full of dirt; dirt stuck to the sweat on his back and smudged across his cheeks and forehead. Grunt, heave, hack. The dirt cleaved away in dark, cool cuts. He dug faster and faster, until eventually he tossed the shovel, fell to his knees, and dug with his hands. We crawled closer, unnoticed, until we could see the bobbing shape of his head and shoulders as he scooped and flung dirt from the hole. He dug until he could barely breathe, until he collapsed, wheezing, in the dirt.

We walked over and stood around the edge and peered down inside.

"I'll never get out of here," Paps said. The dirt had crumbled down and powdered him brown all over, except for the blood that was seeping from his knuckles and the tips of his fingers, and the red of his mouth, which was busy licking and spitting dirt and breathing hard. I wasn't sure if he meant he couldn't get up out of the hole he had dug, or if he was trying to escape our yard through a tunnel to somewhere else, like China.

Joel must have thought the same thing, because he asked, "Where you trying to get to?" But Manny only flicked his ear and called him a dipshit.

"Give your ol' man a hand, why don't ya?"

We lay down on the grass outside the hole and took hold of his wrists and tugged and tugged, but he didn't budge; instead he pulled us in with him and held us there in his big arms, us laughing and screaming and flailing about. We kicked the walls of the hole, and more dirt rained in, so that everyone was spitting and choking, but no one could get away — he was a strong man, our Paps, and he knew just how to hold on to all three at once.

When we were finally outside the hole, Paps slapped at himself, dusting the dirt from his clothes. We followed him back into the house, sneaking up and slapping him on the ass, over and over, yelling, "You missed a spot! You missed a spot!" He shook his fist and took a couple of blind swings, but he didn't hit us.

"Be good," he said. "I'm going to pick your mother up from work." But he must have gotten distracted by something on the way to the brewery, because Ma came home hours later — she had worked through the night, and now it was a little after noon, and she was all alone and drunk and mad as hell.

"Where is he? Where's the truck?" She looked at each one of us, at our empty faces, then she closed her eyes and leaned against the wall and slid down to the floor. She unlaced her steel-toed boots and hurled them across the room.

"He dug a trench," Joel said.

Ma took pains peeling down her white socks. Little bits of white lint stuck to her feet, and she blew them away with long, drawn-out gusts. She focused all of her attention on the process, like she was unwrapping a fragile mummy. She curled and uncurled her toes. Then she began on the buttons of her heavy cotton men's shirt, which had her name embroidered onto a tag on the front.

"A trench?"

"Out back."

"What do you know about trenches?" Ma asked, wrestling with her buttons.

"Joel thinks it's a grave," I said and felt Joel's fist hit the small of my back.

Ma stopped and looked at each one of our faces. Her shirttails were pulled out and unbuttoned from the bottom, splitting open toward her heart.

"Naps," she said, "all of you. Right now."

We didn't sleep. We lay, the three of us in one bed, fanning ourselves with paper fans, our black polish melting in the sweat. We listened to Ma in the kitchen, opening and closing the cupboards. Joel joked about her painted toenails, their pinkness wrapped up inside those sweat socks and work boots all day.

"You see how excited she is to come home and see them toes again?" he asked. "She's toe proud. Toe crazy."

The back door creaked open and we went to the window. We didn't risk leaning out, but we could see Ma clear enough. She was standing at the edge of the hole, smoking and peering down inside. Then she stepped in and disappeared from view; she lay herself down in that hole, and not more than a minute later, the sky cracked, and the rain dropped down — pouring rain, sheets of it sliding down the window like at the car wash.

"It's like she did that," Manny whispered.

"Did what?"

"Made it rain."

"Shut up."

"That hole's magic."

We went to the bathroom and grabbed two towels off the floor, then sat at the kitchen table and waited until Ma came in, streaked with mud, her hair wet and webbed across her forehead. She plopped her clothes onto the linoleum. She wasn't crying, and she wasn't angry to see us up out of bed. She took the towels and covered herself, and we followed her into the living room, where she sighed and fell down onto the couch. We got more towels and swiped at the leftover mud and wet. When we ran out, we used paper napkins until she was as clean and dry as we could get her, then we covered her with a blanket.

"Does he think I'll just take this?" she asked, but she wasn't asking us.

Sitting on the floor in front of the couch, with our knees held to our chests, we dared each other to go out into the hole. The rain had tapered off, a summer storm, but it would still be wet, and in our imagination the hole had filled up with worms and maggots and drowned moles. We had decided not to let Paps near her, not today — we had plastic guns and camo, we were Ma's militia — so we could go out to the hole only one at a time.

Manny was first. He came back mud slicked like Ma, but we didn't move to help him clean up.

"That's a magic hole," he said, smiling. He shook like a dog and sprinkled us with filth. Joel, of course, didn't believe Manny's magic-hole bullshit, but he spent a long time out there, longer than Manny, and when he came back, his clothes were dry.

"What'd you take your clothes off or something?" Manny asked.

"Sure I did."

"And?"

Joel shrugged. "Could be. Could be magic. We'll see."

I was squeamish about mud, and even though the day was muggy and hot, I thought the mud in the hole would be cold, and I was squeamish about that as well, and worms — I could see one worm, and I knew there would be more. I took off my clothes like Joel had, all of them, and once I was naked there was nothing for it but to climb in.

It was a grave. It was my grave. Paps had dug my grave. Those were my first thoughts, and when I was fully horizontal, half submerged in puddle muck, stories about people being buried alive rushed into my mind — avalanches, mudslides, suffocation — but I had a wish, and so I stayed to wish it. I could see a squarish patch of sky, framed by the walls of the hole, and that sky calmed me some, the clouds, the blue; it would not rain again today. I felt a great distance from the house, from Ma on the couch and my brothers and Paps. The clouds seemed to move faster than I had ever known them to, and if I concentrated, if I let go enough, an understanding would blur inside of me and I could trick my body into feeling that it was moving and the clouds were still — and then I was certain that I was moving, and the hole was magic. I closed my eyes and stayed quiet and motionless but felt movement, sometimes sinking, sometimes floating away, or stretching or shrinking. I allowed myself to lose all bearings, and a long, long time passed before I wished my wish.

What pulled me out was their laughter. All four of them, Ma and Manny and Joel and Paps, growing up out of the mud above me and swaying with laughter, like trees. My brothers grabbed each other's shoulders and shook and pointed, weeping with laughter, saying, "Look at him, just look at him! Just look at that baby!"

And Ma was saying that it was OK, that I could come out now. "You come on out of that trench," she was saying.

And Paps was leaning down and reaching to help me up; he was telling me that the war was over.

TRASH KITES

W E WALKED FOR MILES, the three of us, kicking up gravel, dragging sticks behind us. We were sneaking out; we were finding freedom. Above us, naked branches stretched into shadows and the sky deepened, wrapping itself up in a shroud of dark purple. It was getting colder, and Joel and I wondered out loud if maybe we should turn back.

"We're on a good path," Manny said, "we're doing right, we're safe."

We reached an empty field, tossed our backpacks onto the grass, and set up camp. Wind whipped the tips of our ears and stole a plastic bag right out of Manny's hand. He thought it was a sign and fished through our supplies until he pulled out a tight, fat roll of twine and three black plastic bags. We made kites: trash bags on strings. We ran, slipped, the knees of our dungarees all grass stained, we got up, ran, choked ourselves half to death with laughter, but we found speed, and our trash kites soared. We flew for an hour or so, until daylight fully buried itself into night and all the light sank back, except for the stars and a toenail clipping of moon, and the kites disappeared, black on blackness. That's when we let go, and our trash kites really soared — up and away, heavenward, like prayers, our hearts chasing after.

Paps came crunching down the road with his high beams on — our sleeping bags and backpacks and our shielded faces all caught in his searchlight.

"Fuck," Manny said, "we should have slept in the woods." But probably Paps would have hunted us down anyway. He was like that; he knew tricks for tracking down people who didn't want to be found.

Paps assumed it was all Manny's idea because Manny was the oldest and because it was, actually, all Manny's idea. He didn't wait to get home but beat Manny right there in the field, the headlights scaling back the night, casting long wild shadows on the trees, the engine running and the door left wide open, so that the inside of the car was perfectly lit and I could see, from twenty feet away, moths fluttering in and bumping into one another. He beat Manny bad; punched his face, punched his crotch. Manny went crazy, hooting and hollering "Murderer!" over and over.

"Murderer!" he screamed at our father, but no one was dead. He crawled over to where I stood, grabbed my sleeve, looked into my eyes. "Murderer!" he said.

"But who's dead?"

"Me," he said. "Me, I'm dead! And my children."

Manny was always saying all kinds of crazy shit, most of

it to me, because Joel had a way of closing himself off from crazy, but I couldn't figure out how to stop from hearing his words and howls, how to look away.

So later that night, back at home, just before dawn, Manny climbed into my bed and woke me up, telling me how he had dreamt of kites — a whole sky full of kites, and he was holding all the strings. He told me how the good kites and wicked kites got all mixed up, how he tried to hold on to the good and let the rest float away, but after a while he couldn't tell them apart.

I didn't say anything. We were on our backs, not touching, but I could tell he was holding himself tight, every little muscle tight. I thought he might cry, or scream. I thought he might climb up on top of me.

"Paps apologized, you know," Manny said, "for using his fists. He told me he was scared, that something serious could have happened to us."

He rolled onto his side and watched my face. I pretended to yawn; I didn't like his eyes on me.

"I used to believe we could escape," he whispered. "I had it all figured out — like when we were in the field today, I was sure that God would grab hold of those kites and lift us up, protect us."

He took my chin and turned my face toward his.

"But now I know," he said, "God's scattered all the clean among the dirty. You and me and Joel, we're nothing more than a fistful of seed that God tossed into the mud and horseshit. We're on our own."

He wrapped one arm and one leg around me and was silent and still for a stretch of time, and I drifted into sleep. After a while Manny started up again, talking to himself, plotting, saying, "What we gotta do is, we gotta figure out a way to reverse gravity, so that we all fall upward, through the clouds and sky, all the way to heaven," and as he said the words, the picture formed in my mind: my brothers and me, flailing our arms, rising, the world telescoping away, falling up past the stars, through space and blackness, floating upward, until we were safe as seed wrapped up in the fist of God.

WASN'T NO ONE
TO STOP THIS

I N THE EVENING, we drew a chalk circle in the street and divided the circle into three sections. We had a blue rubber ball, and we each stood in one of the sections and smacked the ball with our palms, from one to the other, trying to keep the ball alive. With each smack, we imitated our Paps.

"This is for raising your voice —"

"And this is for embarrassing me in public —"

"And this is for doing something —"

"And this is for doing nothing —"

"And this —"

There was the gutter, which caught the ball when we missed, and there were cars that came fast around the bend, then slowed upon seeing us. We stood to the side of the road and looked hard at the drivers through the glass as they passed. If there were kids in the cars, we showed them our tongues or our middle fingers. We had nylon fall jackets, windbreakers with collapsible hoods that rolled up and zipped into the neck like a parachute. We had our blue ball and our anger and the evening sky moving into twilight and the peaks of the roofs against that darkening sky, the antennae, the telephone cables, and somewhere we had a crow calling.

Manny said, "There's white magic and there's black magic," and we believed him.

Lately, Manny was always trying to explain to Joel and me about God. He led us out into the woods and had us hunt for mushrooms, poisonous mushrooms, put on earth by God to work his black magic. There were white mushrooms with oily black undersides and flat, rippled mushrooms clinging to rotted-out logs, and mushrooms that puffed out a yellow smoke of spores when squeezed, but none of them contained God's black magic, and then the last of the light was gone, and all was dark.

We were cold, but we wouldn't go home yet. There had been other children earlier; they kept separate from us, but we heard them playing in the street, and we heard as they were called inside one by one for supper. I was afraid of the dark, but no one knew; I'd never spoken the fear. I was afraid of black magic; I was afraid of poison — and when Manny and Joel decided to see who could throw the rubber ball hard enough to break the window of the Grices' camper, which had been parked in the same spot for as long as we could remember, two wheels holding up the back and the front supported by a stack of grayed lumber—I was afraid we'd be punished, but I kept my mouth shut.

The ball thudded against the glass and rolled back toward where we crouched at the edge of the woods. A light flicked on in a back room of the house.

"They can't see shit out here, they can't see us."

We waited, and after a short time the light shut.

"Use a rock this time," Joel said to Manny.

"Let's just wait a minute, or else they'll get suspicious."

We crouched in the dirt and smelled the air. With the backs of our hands, we rubbed life into the tips of our noses. We sucked back snot. After a while Joel mumbled, "It's fucking cold," because someone had to say the obvious so that the other two could ignore him, and in this way we knew that no one wanted to go home. A while after that, Manny said, "White magic is like rabbits in hats and shit, card tricks, whatever."

The earth was hard and cool where we crouched, just damp enough to stick to our knees and the balls of our hands. The dirt squeezed up shut in the winter and softened in the summer, and autumn dirt was my favorite dirt, like cooled black coffee grinds. Black magic.

"Black magic is voodoo, snake-charming, poison," Manny said. "You could kill someone with black magic."

Manny threw the rock, and then we were running, at the full speed of terror, along the edge of the woods, running, running, running, falling down and catching our breath, with the sound of the shattering glass playing over and over in our minds, the sound of permanence, the delightful, shocking sound of damage done.

We turned back and watched the Grices' house to see if we were being followed, and sure enough the Grices' son, the headbanger, appeared — two years older than Manny and stick thin. He walked down the middle of the street, swinging a flashlight at his side. When he came to the spot where we had drawn our chalk circle, he stopped and ran his light along the circle's outside edge. He raised the light higher in the air so he could see the drawing in its entirety. Then he kept walking down the road toward the dead end where we crouched at the woods' edge.

"Boys," he sang, "boyyyys."

Manny got up and walked to the log that marked the end of the road and sat, so that the headbanger would see Manny when he arrived — see that Manny wasn't hiding. Joel and I followed, swiping the dirt from our knees and rubbing our palms.

"Three dogs on a log," the boy said and swept the light back and forth across us. We shielded our eyes. The Dead End sign glowed yellow in the flashlight's reflection, and the headbanger held the light there and laughed.

"Everything's diffcrent in the dark," he said, then switched off the light and joined us on the log, dogged with us.

"Well, hiya, fellas. How you fellas doin'?"

He knew it was us who had just broken the window on that old camper — that much was obvious — and there was an odd humor in his voice. The headbanger had been sniffing around us lately, trying to joke with us; we didn't know why; could be nothing more than we were the only ones near his age who were still out well past supper, could be something meaner. He came from up north, he claimed, from Texas, from California. Blond-white hair fell long and stringy down his back but was cut short at the sides and front. He was always pulling at his crotch and telling as many lies as he could cram into a sentence. This type of boy was everywhere around us, but mostly we kept separate, us three half-breeds in our world, and the white-trash boys in theirs. We had been as warned against them as they had against us, and besides, we didn't need them; we had each other for games and hunts and scraps. We still ran thick; Manny up front, making rules, and Joel to break all of them, and me keeping the peace as best I could, which sometimes meant nothing more than falling down to my knees and covering my head with my arms and letting them swing and cuss until they got tired, or bored, or remorseful. They called me a faggot, a pest, left me black and blue, but they were gentler with me than they were with each other. And everyone in the neighborhood knew: they'd bleed for me, my brothers, had bled for me.

And then this headbanger swooped in with his "Hiya, fellas" and tore us open, thinned what was thick.

And not even from our block, just moseying up the street with one hand stuffed into his pocket, pulling on his crotch from inside his dungarees. "I said, 'Hiya, fellas,' can't you talk?"

And Manny, "What you want?"

And Joel, "Yeah, what you want anyway?"

And this headbanger, "I want to show you something. I got something good to show and nobody to show it to."

"You talking about black magic?" Joel asked.

"Shut up, Joel," said Manny.

I waited for Manny to tell the headbanger to get the hell off our log, off our block; I waited for Manny to turn back to us, to turn his back fully on the headbanger, call him a clown, then turn to us and say, "OK, this is what's up for tonight, you listening?"

But Manny kept his head forward.

"What you got?" he asked the headbanger.

And Joel, "Yeah, what you got, anyway?"

The headbanger stood and clicked on the flashlight and said, "Come here."

We followed him to the road, and he raised the flashlight high on our sectioned chalk circle as he had before, so that all of it was illuminated.

"You know what this means?"

There were the crickets and the lights in the windows of all the houses. We were cold. I put my thumb in my mouth and tasted the dirt.

"Peace," the headbanger said, "this here's a sign of peace."

Manny laughed, a knowing puff of air through his nose, then he bent his head back, raised his gaze from the pavement to the stars, right up into God's eyes. Lately, Manny looked out, looked up, looked into everyone and everything, not just us.

And then this headbanger said, "I got something else to show you. Something good. Better."

"That right?" Manny asked.

And so we followed him home.

In the front room, the headbanger's father smoked, washed in blue from the light of the television, one hand tucked into his armpit.

"They know what time it is?" he said to the headbanger as we filed into the house and past the television, our shadows sliding over him.

"They know."

In the kitchen, I rubbed my hands all over the table, which was smooth and lacquered and cool. The headbanger set out plastic cups of pop for us, and Manny and Joel drank in a too-fast way that made me nervous, gasping for breath between gulps. The father shut the television, and the noise of the crickets rushed in. The headbanger squinted and listened, not for the crickets, but for the father, for his next move. We knew that squint; what stunned us was the way the headbanger was moving his lips — wild, without voice. He was animal-eyed and white-haired and he stunned us. Without his voice, the headbanger told us not to move, or he prayed, or he cursed his father, a black magic voodoo curse, or he did all of those things at once, just by moving his lips, this kid.

We listened to the father stomp up the stairs and into the bedroom. A door slammed shut, and then another TV started up. I fumbled my cup, and the pop ran to the slit in the middle of the table and made a noise as it fell, exactly like someone pissing on the floor.

"Leave it," the headbanger said, opening the basement door and summoning us over with a curled finger.

We made the headbanger switch on the fluorescent light and go down the stairs in front of us. We took three steps, then bent, looked all over for traps, weapons, other kids. We took three more steps, paused. Manny said, "You sleep down here?"

"Upstairs."

"Shit smells."

"It's a basement, what do you want? You fellas chicken-shit or something? Ain't you never been in a basement?"

"Sure I have," Manny said.

"We all have," said Joel. "Together. The three of us. Plenty of times."

But the headbanger wasn't listening; he had moved to a chest and was pulling out a blanket.

Three steel posts held up the floor of the house above. The ceiling was striped with rolls of insulation nailed to the underside of the floor with a nail gun, and one long strip had unpeeled itself, or been torn down, and now kissed the basement's dirt floor. The tuft of fiberglass was thick and pink and exposed. The headbanger led us to a corner room, sectioned off by three flaking wooden shutters. A gap between two of the shutters functioned as a doorway, and for the door there was a bed sheet patterned with winged helmets.

Inside this room sat an old console television and a VCR.

"I'm getting a couch," the headbanger said as he unfurled a ratty tiger-shaped throw onto the floor. Dust flew up and hung in the dank air, and we fanned our hands in front of our noses and coughed. From the hind waistband of his dungarees, hidden under his shirt, the headbanger produced a black plastic rectangle, a VCR tape, and displayed the tape with both hands in front of him, like a steering wheel. The title had been inked out with black marker.

"This is it," he said, "this is what I wanted to show you."

The tape began, the image rolled a few times over the screen, then settled and sharpened. A white kid, a teenager, was on a bed, turning the pages of a book. There was a knock on the door, and an older man entered; he called him Dad.

"Dad," he said, "what do you want?"

"I want to know how come you haven't done the dishes like I told you."

One time, months ago, at the public pool, a mother, talking distractedly to her daughter, who was probably five or six, took a left instead of a right, and walked into the men's changing room, where my brothers, my father, myself, and other men and boys were showering, changing, clothed and naked. The mother had flushed and covered her daughter's eyes, instinctively; she had put both hands over her daughter's face and hustled her from the locker room. And the men — who never looked at nor spoke to each other outside their own kin — the men had suddenly looked around from one to the next, and after a pause, they had all erupted in laughter.

"*My goodness*," the mother had said, just before grabbing the girl and shielding her eyes. "*My goodness*." I remembered that.

And the TV, "Aw shucks, Daddy, leave me alone!"

And the TV, "Don't you talk back to me."

We sat on the tiger, each of us holding our knees in the crooks of our elbows — sucker-punched, hypnotized. There was the musty smell, the dirt underneath. There was the headbanger, who had been whistling, claiming, "You never seen a tape like this, I'll bet you never" — now gone quiet, mouth breathing. A film of sweat seeped over my palms, and with the sweat came heat and nausea. There was white magic and there was black magic.

And the TV, "Aw, I didn't mean nothing by it!"

Our Paps didn't truck in pornography; he had told us so and told the truth; if he had dirty tapes or pictures, we would have found them. Once, at a garage sale, we had come across a cardboard box with Adults Only scrawled across.

The old man had laughed at us from his lawn chair. "You go on ahead," he had said, "but you see a lady stop by to have a look at my dishes, you just step on away from that box."

We had seen flesh, women, sex parts, and sex acts, but only in still pictures. This man, this teenager, they were alive, or had been once — in this sparse room, just a bed, sheets, a book, one continuous shot, no angles, no cutting away, like a home movie.

"You're going to learn your lesson, young man."

My goodness, the mother had said, in the locker room, as if her goodness was a special treat stolen out of her hands by a naughty bird.

"Pull down your underwear."

I had seen mothers cover the ears of their children when someone was cussing or when the mothers needed to cuss themselves. And I had seen a woman cover a child's ears when another spoke against God.

"Bend over my lap."

Wasn't no one to stop this. My brothers. Wasn't no one.

"Daddy, please."

We had seen flesh, but still pictures, women. And, too, we had seen each other's bodies — all of us, me and Manny and Joel, Ma and Paps — we had seen one another beaten, animal bleating in pain, hysterical, and now drugged, and now drunk and glazed, and naked, and joyous, heard high laughter, squeals and tears, and we had seen each other proud, empty proud, spite proud, and also trampled, also despised. We boys, we had always seen so much of them, penniless or flush, in and out of love with us, trying, trying; we had seen them fail, but without understanding, we had taken the failing, taken it wide-eyed, shameless, without any sense of shame.

"This is for —"

Wasn't none of it nothing like this.

"And this is for —"

Wasn't us. Didn't have nothing to do with us.

"Yeah, you like that, don't you."

Why won't you look at me, my brothers, why won't you take my eyes?

NIAGARA

MANNY AND JOEL were flunking, so when a man
paid my father to drive a package up to Niagara
Falls, it was me Paps took out of school for two days; it was
me he brought along for company. We drove for four hours;
Paps didn't say much, just that we were headed east, around
Lake Ontario, hugging the shore. We stayed in a dusty mo-
tel room, and in the morning Paps took me to see the falls,
and there, at the rustling and noisy edge, he hoisted me into
the air and folded me across the railing so that my torso was
suspended above the thick gushing cords of water and the
mist was kissing me all over my neck and face, and when I
didn't kick or scream, he leaned me out farther and he put
his lips to my ear and he said, "Do you know what would
happen if I let you go?"

And I said, "What?"

And he said, "You'd die."

The water was tripping over itself, splashing and hypnotizing, and I tried to fix my mind on a chunk of it, like each little ripple was a life that began far away in a high mountain source and had traveled miles pushing forward until it arrived at this spot before my eyes, and now without hesitation that water-life was hurling itself over the cliff. I wanted my body in all that swiftness; I wanted to feel the slip and pull of the currents and be dashed and pummeled on the rocks below, and I wanted him to let me go and to die.

Later, Paps pulled up to a little museum of curiosities and handed me a five-dollar bill and told me he'd be back in an hour to pick me up.

"What happens when you die?" I asked.

"Nothing happens," he said. "Nothing happens forever."

The museum had wax replicas of freakish heads — people born with two pupils to each eye or forked tongues — and old sepia pictures of Siamese twins and babies with tails. There was a small room with a low ceiling and a bench where a three-minute film was being projected on a loop. The film showed men in barrels, smiling and waving and giving the thumbs-up to the camera as they approached the falls and then disappearing over its sudden edge. *While some of these daredevils miraculously survived,* the narrator droned, *many more met their tragic ends.*

Hours passed. A man came by twice and poked his head into my theater and looked at me questioningly. The third time, he came in and sat next to me and asked, "How many times you plan on watching this crap?"

I shrugged my shoulders. He was wearing corduroy pants, and I would have liked to drag my fingernail across his thigh.

"You hiding?"

"I'm just sitting here," I said.

"Yeah, never mind," he said. "I guess you're a bit young for that. What about your folks?"

"My father's coming to get me. He should be here any minute."

The man stood up and looked down at me. The film projected across his shirt and cut him off at the waist, so that he looked like a giant, rising up out of the great Niagara.

"You tell your father to come and see me in the ticket booth when he shows up. I'd like to meet him."

When he left, I stood where he had been, and the waterfall projected across my face and arms. I moved closer to the wall so that the waterfall swallowed me up and I danced. I pretended I was a mer-boy prince and it was my job to try and catch all the men in barrels and save them from their deaths, but when I cupped my hands and reached up, they always slipped through. When they disappeared over the edge, I danced a special underwater dance, so that their souls could go up to heaven. Soon I stopped trying to save them at all because I was consumed in the death dance; spinning on my toes and looking down at my body, the water slipping and rushing over me, I slithered my arms and wiggled my hips against the current.

When I looked up, Paps was in the doorway, watching

me. His arms were raised, resting on the top of the door frame, and the light poured in behind him, obscuring his expression from me, but I knew from his silhouetted muscles and close-cropped Afro that it was him, and I knew too that he had been standing there, watching me, for some time. He dragged his hands down the sides of the doorway and then slapped them against his legs.

"Let's get out of here," he said.

Out on the sidewalk, I looked behind us, half expecting the man in the corduroy pants to be running after, but we were alone.

We ate at a counter with spinning vinyl stools. We both had hot dogs; Paps broke his in half and stuffed an entire half into his mouth, then turned to look at me — his eyes wide and his cheeks bulging. I didn't laugh; he had left me there, alone, for too long.

It was dark by the time we got on the road. We drove all night. Paps said he was exhausted and it was my job to keep him awake. He kept yawning and yawning, and I stared up at his profile, watching his eyelid grow heavy and droop and finally close, then I'd grab his arm and shake him, and he'd say, "What? What happened?"

We didn't speak. I knew he was in a faraway world, half dreaming. When we pulled off the highway and onto the road that would bring us home, he said, "Yeah, it's a funny thing." He said it out of nowhere, as if we had been in conversation the entire time.

"I stood in that doorway, watching you dance, and you

know what I was thinking?" He paused, but I didn't answer or turn to look at him; instead I closed my eyes.

"I was thinking how pretty you were," he said. "Now, isn't that an odd thing for a father to think about his son? But that's what it was. I was standing there, watching you dance and twirl and move like that, and I was thinking to myself, *Goddamn, I got me a pretty one.*"

THE NIGHT I AM MADE

THEY GREW UP wiry, long-torsoed, and lean. Their kneecaps, their muscles, bulged like knots on a rope. Broad foreheads and strong ridges along the brow announced their resemblance. Their cheeks hollowed, their lips barely covered their teeth and gums, as if the jaw and the skull inside wanted out.

They hunched and they skulked. They jittered. They scratched.

Out on the loading dock, in the lamplight, they watched the night. They watched their breath chill before them and float out into the cold dark. They stood hoodless in the snow, pinching the cotton filters from their cigarettes. They talked about breaking and entering. They loved to say about a thing that it was laced — their night, their drugs. Later, one of them will smash his face into the locker-room mirror over a girl, another will slice up his arms. They'll flunk. They'll roll one car after another into a ditch. Later they'll truck in all manner of pornography. Soon they'll drop out. At work, they'll fall in with all the other boys like them, boys with punched-out teeth, bad breath, easy winks. They'll skunk around in basement apartments with grown men who keep pet snakes in glass aquariums. Later still, they'll realize that those boys are actually nothing like them at all. Who knows this mutt life, this race mixing? Who knows Paps? All these other boys, the white trash out here, they have legacies, decades upon decades of poverty and violence and bloodlines they can trace like a scar; and these are their creeks, their hills, their goodness. Their grandfathers poured the cement of this loading dock. And downstate, in Brooklyn, the Puerto Ricans have language, they have *language*.

Later, they'll see, ain't no other boys as pitiless, as new, as orphaned.

But out on that loading dock, they looked into the future and saw otherwise.

They felt proud to be the kind of boys they were — boys who spat in public, boys who kept their gaze on the floor or fixed on a space above your head, boys who looked you in the eye only to size you up or scare you off. When they bit the chapped skin from their lower lips, when they chewed up the web between thumb and pointer, when they scratched inside their ears with house keys, they were looking at memories, proud memories, blood memories, or else they were dreaming about their wild futures. Out on that loading dock they chanted, *Nah, man, Get out of here with that shit, Fuck that, Let me tell you how it was, Let me tell you how it's gonna be.*

They weren't scared, or dispossessed, or fragile. They were possible. Soon they'd be sailing right over them ditches. Soon they'd be handling that cash. They'd decide. They'd forge themselves consequential. They'd sing the mixed breed.

And me now. Look at me. See me there with them, in the snow — both inside and outside their understanding. See how I made them uneasy. They smelled my difference — my sharp, sad, pansy scent. They believed I would know a world larger than their own. They hated me for my good grades, for my white ways. All at once they were disgusted, and jealous, and deeply protective, and deeply proud.

Look at us, our last night together, when we were brothers still.

MIDNIGHT

WE FINISHED OFF the liquor, hopped down from the dock, and Manny tossed the empty bottle Hail Mary into the line of trees. We didn't hear it come down, we didn't hear a single rustle or thud — and we reveled in the joy of this silent miracle. Manny invented a black hole; Joel suggested that the bottle landed perfectly in a raccoon's yawning mouth; I just razzed, *That's the stupidest bullshit I ever heard.* We stepped into our shadows and the echoes of our laughter, headed nowhere. The alcohol warmed our bellies; the snowflakes thickened the air before us.

Around the corner there was the four-barreled steel Dumpster, and in the Dumpster's shelter hid the eight-nippled stray cat. We dug into our pockets for milk money; Manny had seventy-five cents. Fifteen minutes' walk to the gas station, no one was cold. At the counter we slid the change to the attendant, a Near Eastern man the hue and hulk of our Paps.

"You could be our father," I said, and Manny and Joel busted up into coughing laughter.

The man looked at our coins. "You're short."

We patted pockets, pretended to fish, came up empty. The lights inside cut into our smooth buzz; the counter's veneer had been coin-rubbed raw. This man wasn't nothing like our Paps.

"Go on, take it," he said. "Get out of here."

So we ambled back to our stray, grabbing at whatever we found along the shoulder and tossing it into the trees. If something—a rock, a flank of rubber—landed without making a sound, we erupted into cheers. Sometimes we pretended not to have heard the crashing; we cheered on anyway.

For a milk bowl we used the plastic lid of a five-gallon tub and the milk thinned into a shallow layer. Didn't look like much. Our stray barely raised her muzzle to sniff the air.

"She'll eat later," Joel said, "when we're gone."

This was our own Ma's pledge, when we used to worry for her.

The kittens clawed and pushed in the suckling pile; some seemed to be asleep at the tit; they were ugly, desperate things.

"How long before them kittens forget they're kin, start fighting and fucking each other?" Manny asked. "How long before they jump the runt?"

They both sniggered, and they were sniggering at me, the fay, the runt of our litter; we were once those kittens—three thick, three warm. And we blood-fought over a tin can of pet milk. And jump the runt was a trick mean as any they pulled on me.

"Fuck you," I said. I hadn't drunk half as much as either one of them—I took hesitant swigs or kept my lips closed and only pretended. But still I had drunk enough to be surprised at the sound of my own voice, and at the venom. "And fuck this creeping around. What are we doing out here anyway?"

"Hey now," said Joel.

"Chill," said Manny. "You're twisting up your panties."

They snorted out little chuckles from their noses.

"I'm tired of this. This is bullshit. This creeping around."

"Who's creeping?" asked Manny. "I'm just standing here."

"You're a creep," I said. "Look in the mirror. Can you even see yourself? You're always going on about God. And then the next minute you're talking about hos. As if you know shit about either one — as if God wasn't as disgusted by you as girls are."

"Oh shit!" said Joel, delighted.

"What, that makes you happy?"

"Kind of," Joel replied.

"Kind of," I mimicked. "You are so fucking ignorant. You embarrass me. Did you know that? That you embarrass me?"

"You hear that?" Manny said to Joel. "We embarrass him."

Look at my brothers — their saggy clothes, their eyes circled dark like permanent bruises, their hangdog hungry faces. I felt trapped and hateful and shamed. Secretly, outside of the family, I cultivated a facility with language and a bitter spite. I kept a journal — in it, I sharpened insults against all of them, my folks, my brothers. I turned new eyes to them, a newly caustic gaze. I sensed a keen power of observation in myself, an intelligence, but sour. Both Ma and Paps had held private conversations with me about my potential, about this bookishness that set me apart from my brothers; both encouraged me to apply myself — they hinted that I would have an easier time in this world than they had, than my brothers would ever have, and I hated them for that.

But the worst was pity.

"You know what? Forget it," I said. "Never mind."

They wouldn't abide my pity.

"You're fucked up," said Joel.

Manny scooped down and packed a snowball in his bare hands. He took up a branch, pitched the ball to himself, and whipped the air. The snowball exploded, and we all three watched the effect, a little storm within the storm.

"He's right," Manny said, turning on me in a flush, pointing the branch. "You're fucked up. Admit it."

He held the branch there, an inch from my nose. "Admit it."

Then Joel was behind me, locking my arms in a full nelson. I tried to shrug him off, but it was no use. They were both drunk; Manny held that damn branch right in front of my face. I imagined the welt of it slamming across the side of my head. And I wanted it.

"Either you're fucked up, or you're getting fucked up. Which one will it be?"

Look at us three, look at how they held me there — they didn't want to let me go.

"Go ahead, Manny, beat me with that stick. See if it makes you feel better." My voice started strong but ended soft, a whisper, a plea. "Just fucking beat me with it."

Manny pumped two fake swings; I flinched each time. Then he sighed in disgust, and Joel slacked off his grip. The stick dropped.

"Seriously," Manny said, quieter now, "you're acting fucked up. There is something seriously fucking wrong with you in the head. Let's talk about *that*."

But we didn't. We couldn't.

We let the snow fall on us some more, white piled up on our hair, our heads like miniature mountains, until finally, in silence, we agreed to move into the shelter of the building's eave. Manny distributed a cigarette each to Joel and me, and we went about pulling out the filter. Still no one spoke, but the ritual eased the air between us — the spark of fire, the noisy exhalations, our little clouds of smoke.

Then, slowly, the jokes and shit talking picked up again, and I waited on the edges, as always, until Manny turned to address me.

"You know what she said to me the other day?"

I didn't ask who, because I knew who.

"She said you were capable of anything."

"Yep," said Joel, "she said some shit like that to me."

"She said you were so bright."

"So bright!"

"And you know what else? She said you were capable of destroying yourself."

"The way she talks about you," Joel said, "like you're a fucking crystal vase."

Manny roped his arm around Joel's neck. "In her mind, we're two of a kind." He pointed at me. "And you, you're —"

"A fucking golden egg."

"She wants us to protect you from the other kids."

Joel laughed. "Right? I told her it ain't like we're all still playing in the same goddamn sandbox, woman."

"And to protect you from yourself."

"It ain't like we're little boys."

"'He's still your little brother,' she says, 'he'll always be your little brother.'"

Look at me, how I itched to leave that loading dock; how I itched to leave that snowy hour.

"'Only if he wants to be,' I says."

"Fucking sacred lamb."

I held my hands up in front of me, surrender style, and walked backward, keeping my eyes on them, until I reached the building's edge.

"Where you going, girlie?"

"Where the fuck you think you're going?"

I made it to the corner and turned, down the sloping path, away from their taunts. They called out after me, putting an angry question mark at the end of my name. Their voices boomed huge in the dark cold air — like waves pounding me from behind.

They called and called and cackled, and the trees echoed with their noise.

Shit, let them bark.

Maybe it was true. Maybe there was no other boy like me, anywhere.

LATE NIGHT

I SLIPPED AWAY and walked the three miles to the bus station. Snow fell gently and swiftly, and when I looked behind me, my tracks were already snow-covered. This was what I'd been up to behind their backs, sleazing around the bus station's men's room. This was the scent they'd picked up.

I left the road and took a footpath that had been trampled through a hedge. The path led straight to the back of the bus station. If the lot was full enough, I could emerge from the hedge and walk between two parked buses to the men's room without anyone's seeing. There was no one to explain any of this to me; I figured out the routine on my own, in small, paranoid steps. For weeks I'd been sneaking to this bus station, lurking, indecisive. I hid in the stalls, peeked through the cracks. At the sink, I washed and washed my hands, unable to return the frank stares in the mirror. I didn't know how to show these men I was ready. The closest I came was with a man who held my chin and tilted my face up to meet his and told me I was a cute kid.

"You're a cute kid," he had repeated. "Now get the fuck out of here."

But this night only one bus idled in the lot. The driver inside spotted me and opened the release, and the door made a loud quick fart of pressurized air.

"New York?"

I pointed to the station. "I gotta pee."

"Not in there. Not at this hour."

"Why not?"

The driver ignored me, kept his eyes on the falling flakes. He wore the uniform, blue polyester slacks, a blue wool cardigan with the bus logo embroidered onto a pocket. A middle-aged man thick all over, down to his fingers, one of which he aimed at the windscreen. "Was scheduled to leave an hour ago, but the snow put a stop to that. Some snow this is, though, beautiful."

A blizzard. The air was warm; the flakes were wet and puffed and sticking; they cut in smooth, relentless, gentle diagonals to the ground. My brothers will lose themselves tonight; they'll search for me in the whiteness; they'll drown.

"Is the building closed?"

"Sent everybody waiting for New York on home. You want to go to New York, you come back in the morning. I'll take you there myself."

"No, sir."

"You got to pee so bad you come on up here."

The door sealed behind me, and I stopped on the top step, daring a look into the driver's eyes. He was done pretending. My heart raced; I looked all around for the door's release, but I could not figure it out.

"The bathroom's back there?"

The driver stood up from his seat. I held there for him, still. I wanted this.

Cold thick fingers wormed past my waistband; I held

still. "You want me to make you," the driver said. "I'll make you. I'll make you."

And I was made.

I trudged back in the predawn. The winter sky was clouded over, all pink gloom. I wanted to look at myself as he had; I wanted to see my black curls peeking out from under my ski cap. What did he make of my thin chest? What did he make of my too-wide smile? He had blasted the heat, but the cold clung and hovered at the back of the bus. The cold gathered in the tips of those fingers, so everywhere he touched me was a dull stab of surprise. I wanted to stand before a mirror and look and look at myself. I opened my mouth and stretched my voice over the buzz of passing cars.

"He made me!" I screamed.

"I'm made!"

DEEP NIGHT

THEY WERE GATHERED in the front room, and the air reeked of grief. The force of their eight eyes pushed me backward toward the door; never had I been looked at with such ferocity. Everything easy between me and my brothers and my mother and my father was lost.

My brothers were still in their jackets, their hair slick with wet, Paps was dressed and shaven, and Ma looked up at me with mascara tiger-striped down her face, raw eyes, hands in her hair — how many times had I seen her like this? She spoke, but I didn't catch what she was saying because on her lap sat, impossibly, my journal.

In bold and explicit language I had written fantasies about the men I met at the bus station, about what I wanted done to me. I had written a catalog of imagined perversions, a violent pornography with myself at the center, with myself obliterated. And now there it was on my mother's lap.

For a moment my thoughts and fears dimmed to black, my vision blurred — an avalanche began, my gut dropped, my sex dropped, my knees gave way, and I fell onto them, hard.

I knelt, just inside the door, and when I spoke to Ma my voice was calm and assured.

"I'll kill you," I said.

Paps lunged, and my brothers, for the first time in their lives, restrained him. But that restraint shifted before my eyes into an embrace; somehow, at the same time that they were keeping him back, they were supporting him, holding Paps upright, preventing him from sliding to the floor himself, and in that moment I realized that not just Ma, but each and every one of them had read the fantasies and delusions, the truth I had written in my little private book.

Two hours later, I am packed into the car and taken to the psych ward of the general hospital, where I will be turned over to the state and institutionalized. Even later, I will come to doubt whether I ever really believed such a book would not be found — maybe my words were all for them, that they might discover themselves, and discover me.

But before all that, before being strapped to a gurney, before the sedation, before the neutered hostility of the nurses and doctors, let us look at me kneeling on the living room floor: my soft curly black hair, days unwashed; my skin marked with acne, but still burning a youthful glow; my arms extended on either side of me, palms up; my slender fingers, the fingers of a piano man, Ma said; my chin lifted, my eyes on my family, who froze before me like a bronze sculpture of sorrow. Paps had his arms around my brothers' shoulders; he leaned into them, and they kept one hand each on his broad chest; they had grown as tall as he; their bodies were whittled-down versions of his own, our common face; and Ma had risen from her seat; she too had moved over to calm Paps, to place a hand on his chest, to lend her support. Each was radiant, gorgeous. How they posed for me. This was our last time all five in a room together. I could have risen; I believe they would have embraced me.

Instead, I behaved like an animal.

I tried to rip the skin from their faces, and when I couldn't, I tried to rip the skin from my own.

They held me down on the ground; I bucked and spat and screamed my throat raw. I cursed them: we were, all of us, sons of whores, mongrels, our mother fucked a beast. They held me, pinned. At first they defended themselves, cursed me, slapped my face, but the wilder I became, the more they retreated into their love for me. Each of them. I chased them down into that love and challenged it — you morons, you sick fucks, I bet you liked reading it, I bet it excited you. I let the spit fly, nostrils wide — my body spasmed in their grip. My voice spiraled up into coughing hysteria.

I said and did animal, unforgivable things.

What else, but to take me to the zoo?

DAWN

LOOK, A FATHER gently lowers his son, fully clothed, into a tub filling with bathwater. The bathroom is small, no window to the outside, stale air. A mother stands in the doorway like a silent movie actress — she has eight fingers in her mouth and she trembles all over. The father turns to her, places his hands on her wrists, and lowers her arms to her sides, all the while whispering in her ear. The mother takes a deep breath and nods, nods.

Then the father eases her out into the hallway and shuts the door. He licks two fingers and reaches up, unscrewing one of the bulbs in the two-bulb fixture over the mirror.

"I always thought that this bathroom was way too bright."

The boy's chin begins to chatter.

"*Mijo*," he says. "My son. You need a bath."

Watch the father rummage through the cabinet below the small tin sink, looking for a washcloth. He runs the water in the sink until it steams. He whistles. Soap, cloth, steam, foam. He whistles.

Look at the son, lulled by the sounds of him, the ritual: whistle, water, suds, and splash. Now the father lathers the cloth. Now the son can only wait.

"How long's it been since you had a bath?"

The boy turns his head halfway away from him, stares

up at a peeling tongue of paint dangling down from the ceiling.

"How long's it been since I *gave* you a bath?"

The boy closes his eyes. Listen to the slur, the tired confusion in the boy's voice as he asks, "Please, Paps, please. Leave me alone to wash myself."

"Hush," says the father. "Hush. Ain't nobody going to leave you alone. Not when you're all worked up like this."

"I'm an adult," the boy says. "I got rights."

"Everybody's got rights. A man tied to a bed got rights. A man down in a dungeon got rights. A little screaming baby got rights. Yeah, you got rights. What you don't got is power."

Down the hall, the mother opens her son's bedroom door and flicks on the light. Look how she steadies herself against the doorjamb. She whispers aloud to no one, enters.

Inside, the mother runs her hand over the surface of the boy's desk. From the high shelf of the closet she pulls down a canvas duffle bag. All the dresser drawers are empty, so she picks the clothes up off the floor, snaps them straight, and folds them, neat and slow. One by one they go, down into the bag.

Look. The snow is stacked two feet high on the roof of the house. Somewhere beyond the snow clouds, the sun rises. The light is stronger every minute. In the driveway, two brothers have started the truck's engine; now they hunch inside the cab. The exhaust billows from the tailpipe and hovers; there is very little wind. No bird song greets the sunrise. Inside, the boys hold their hands in front of the heating vents; they pass a cigarette back and forth in silence. The older boy flicks the knob for the wipers, but they won't respond. The boys look out the windshield onto the gray underlayer of snow. The younger boy stubs the cigarette into the ashtray.

"Well?"

Look. The father lays down the rag, crosses the room, and undresses his son. Cupping and lifting the back of the boy's head with one hand, he tugs his shirt up from his waist and exposes the boy's chest. He lays him back down, lifts his arms, and pulls the wet shirt the rest of the way off. Then he wrestles down the soaking jeans and fishes out one ankle, then the next.

"Paps," says the boy.

The father pulls down the boy's underwear, and he is naked. The father takes him in, stares. Look at the boy, naked from head to foot, searching his father's eyes.

The father squints at the boy, at this nakedness. As if he were looking at a deep cut or a too-bright morning. He calls the boy son again, *Mijo.*

"You smell."

"That ain't me."

The father pushes himself into a laugh, into his role. "That's you, my boy. You're smelling yourself right now."

So the bath begins. Little waterfall flowing down from

the tub's faucet. The rising tide. In the father's pocket sits a nail clipper — it has always been there, since before the boy was born. Look how the father brandishes the clipper, flips open the metal file attachment, and digs and files and clips away dead skin. The boy keeps still and quiet. The father presses the hooked tip into his son's foot until the boy curls his toes and groans.

"Just checking."

Then the washcloth running over the balls of the boy's feet, his heels and ankles, and down the bridge into the crevices between the boy's toes. The boy's feet have not been wet or touched by another in years. The father speaks of cultures where to wash a man's feet is to pay him the ultimate respect, but the boy can only half listen because there is the wet and the cloth and the touch, all of it so brand new and so familiar. Look at him sucking in air, look how the air sticks, a crisp lump in his throat.

The father sits on the edge of the tub, foot in hand, inspecting, rubbing, humming. He takes his time, moving the washcloth slowly up one calf, then the next. There is the wet, the touch. The father stretches his neck and peeks up at his son's face.

"Breathe, boy, just breathe."

Outside the door, the mother listens awhile, then knocks. She calls out the father's name.

"We're getting him fixed up," the father calls back.

Look at how she enters, holding a stack of folded clothes,

jeans on the bottom, a sweatshirt, some boxer shorts, and on top a pair of socks bundled together. Except for her face, her wild, beautiful face, she looks like a servile woman, a television mom.

"The boys are sweeping off the truck," she tells the father. He nods. Hear the way she says it, *the boys*, how quickly and fully the son in the tub is excluded from that designation; how badly the boy wishes to be out there with his brothers, doing as he is told.

The mother sits down on the toilet and watches the father bathe their son. She holds the clothes on her lap. The son will not speak to her. She watches him, and she wants to tell him that he can put all his hate on her; she will take it all, if that's what he needs her to do. Listen, really listen, and that's what she is saying in her silence. The boy can't help but hear.

The father whistles and hums; he is saying goodbye.

"Yes, ma'am," the father says without looking at the mother. "We're going to get him fixed up."

And the mother nods, nods.

The brothers are happy and thankful to have simple work ahead of them — slamming the truck doors with extra force to shake off the snow, scraping the ice from all the windows, pushing the snow from the roof and hood. Their minds are not on the boy and the father in the bathroom. Their minds are not on the mother, crying softly, or the packed duffle bag by the front door. Their minds are on the snow and ice, the simple problem of removal.

And in the tub, the boy is grateful, too, that his brothers have this task. Outside, they have the fresh cold air to clear their throats and noses after being shut up with that cigarette in the cab. In the garage they have aluminum shovels. They can start at the bottom of the driveway and work their way toward the truck, digging down until their shovels hit gravel — the crunch will echo in the silence around them. In work, they can be together, deep inside a chore they've split over many winters. Only the last task, the salting, will bring their minds to the boy in the tub, to the first winter he joined them out there, bundled into a full-body snowsuit. He was too slow and weak with the shovel, so the older brothers gave him a plastic sand bucket full of crystals and ordered him to follow along behind. Now the salting will be split between the two of them. They will pour the bag off into two buckets and scatter the salt across the drive, like seeds or ash. The boy knows that after the shock of this night, his brothers will treat each other formally, with dignity — if one accidentally throws snow in the other's direction, if one nicks the other's heel with his shovel, the guilty one will say *I'm sorry*. Listen and you will hear their whispers floating up toward the house, *I'm sorry, man, I'm sorry*. And a moment later, the refrain, *For nothing, brother, for nothing*.

Look, they're opening doors. They're stepping out. Here they go.

ZOOKEEPING

THESE DAYS, I SLEEP with peacocks, lions, on a bed of leaves. I've lost my pack. I dream of standing upright, of uncurled knuckles, of a simpler life — no hot muzzles, no fangs, no claws, no obscene plumage — strolling gaily, with an upright air.

I sleep with other animals in cages and in dens, down rabbit holes, on tufts of hay. They adorn me, these animals — lay me down, paw me, own me — crown me prince of their rank jungles.

"Upright, upright," I say, I slur, I vow.

ACKNOWLEDGMENTS

Many thanks to United States Artists, the Iowa Writers' Workshop, the Stanford Creative Writing Program, the Ucross Foundation, Lambda Literary, the Truman Capote Literary Trust, and the Tin House and Bread Loaf conferences for their generous support.

Heartfelt thanks to Jin Auh, my agent, and Jenna Johnson, my editor at HMH, for working with me and working so hard for the book.

My favorite hobby is finding teachers to admire, then admiring the hell out of them. Here's a partial list: Dorothy Allison, Lan Samantha Chang, Allan Gurganus, Marilynne Robinson, Stacey D'Erasmo, Michael Cunningham, Paul Harding, Edward Carey, Bret Anthony Johnston, Jeffery Renard Allen, Ann Cummins, Elizabeth Tallent, Adam Johnson, and Tobias Wolff.

Extra special thanks to Laura Iodice, my high school English teacher, who brought me books when I was hospitalized, and whom I love very much.

And to Jackson Taylor, who taught and challenged me. Without your singular and exceptional generosity, Jackson, this book would not exist.

Connie Brothers, Charles Flowers, and Sally Wofford-Girand advised and inspired. And then there are the readers, friends, and heroines: Emma Borges-Scott, Ellie Catton, Angela Flournoy, Kyle McCarthy, Khaliah Williams, Frances Ya-Chu Cowhig, Jennifer De Leon, Kristy Zadrozny, Sara Romano, Marissa Beckett, Casey Romanick, Becky Rotelli, Mary Bates, Ian Gold, Suzy Bentley, Kristina Paiz, Arianna Martinez, Sara Taylor, Adjua Greaves, Karen Good, Joyce Fuller, Valentine Freeman, Adam Gardner, Wei Hwu, Steph Krause, Ade Hall, Sara Minardi, my dear friend Christina Wickens, and the entire Dellios family, but most especially the irreplaceable Olivia Dellios.

Sasha Rodriguez, sister, thank you.

Jaime Shearn Coan, thank you for being an inspiring writer and an incredible friend.

And Ayana Mathis, thank you for reading every draft, every wild incarnation, and patiently, lovingly guiding both me and the book toward realization.

Lastly, vastly, Graham Plumb. I love you.